"I stood pressed against the wall, and the sight below trapped the breath in my throat. Each candle in the chandeliers bloomed like a crocus, each crystal pendant held a rainbow. Light shimmered in the folds of silks and brocade, and laughter and talk floated up to meet the music.

"His hand cradled my elbow, and the curtain dropped behind us, shutting us off from the rest of the world. The moon shone through a side window, paving the floor with pale light. He gently untied the knot of my apron, and it dropped like a tired ghost on a moonlit path...."

How had she, Hester Calladine, been so bold as to love this man who held her now, tenderly, as if fearing his own passion? Yet that day when he had first spoken to her and she had seen the secret anguish in his eyes, she had known that, whatever the odds, she must fight for happiness and a future with the man she loved.

Published by
Dell Publishing Co., Inc.
1 Dag Hammarskjold Plaza
New York, New York 10017

Originally published in Great Britain by
William Heinemann Ltd. under the title *There Is a Season*

Dell ® TM 681510, Dell Publishing Co., Inc.

ISBN: 0-440-18470-3

Printed in the United States of America
First U.S.A. printing—August 1977

So Wild A Love

(*formerly* There Is a Season)

BARBARA BENNETT

A DELL BOOK

To every thing there is a season,
and a time to every purpose under
the heaven.

Ecclesiastes III

So Wild A Love

Another shading, not . . . I'm going to give
you an acre of land and the use of a cow pasture . . .

ONE

I had awakened early that morning, aware that the day was special. I lay beside Matthew listening to his breathing, watching the heaped blankets rise and fall. Still held by sleep, I thought about what the day might bring. Then, from the corner, Daniel's first hunger-wail came, piercing my wooliness, and I realized in that moment what this day would hold. Before it was done we would know what our future was to be.

I lifted him from his crib and stood looking out of the window. In the paling dawn the familiar land lay before me: the garden and, beyond, the Waste—part of the greater countryside, the love of which had earned our king, the third George, the name of 'Farmer.' And this day we were to be told, finally, if we might remain here with the pattern of our days unchanged or if, like so many others in the last few years, we were to lose the small piece of land we'd thought of as ours.

And now, at almost two hours after noon, Matthew stood by the door. The gentle October sunshine edged his dark hair with a rim of gold and lit the bright tips of his thick, stubby lashes. I went over to him and gently re-tied his blue neckcloth. 'It might be good news,' I said, tweaking the ends and smiling. 'Perhaps the Squire's decided to give us all allotments, and when you're gathered in the churchyard he'll tell you so. "Matthew Calladine," he'll say, "I'm going to give you an acre of land and the use of a cow pasture...."'

Smiling, I laid my hands on his thick shoulders, begging a reflection from his set mouth.

'Landowners don't enclose so's to give away land,' he said, morosely. 'They do it to get more.'

'Just the same, there may be a small allotment—even to rent—'

'I'll be surprised if there is.'

'But you don't *know*,' I persisted. 'You don't know *yet*.'

'Reckon I do,' he said. 'And so do you, Hester, deep down. Well . . . I might as well go and hear the worst.'

I curbed my impatience and forced myself to rock Daniel's crib gently. I didn't intend to wait here until Matthew brought the news back. I rocked and rocked, willing Daniel's eyes to close, silently cursing the men who called to each other as they passed on the way to the churchyard. The sooner Daniel slept the sooner I could leave him. And the sooner I could hear the decision that would put an end to all the talk.

The village of Saxtoft had done little but talk ever since that Sunday in September, thirteen months ago, when Sarah Fairchild had come panting across the Waste, shocked by the news but gleeful at being the first to tell it.

'They're going to enclose,' she gasped. 'Squire's going to enclose. It's writ on the church door for everyone to see, and Miss Lacey read it to us this morning.'

We'd half expected it; if tales were true then more land had been enclosed in the past ten years than in any previous such time, so why should we expect Saxtoft to go untouched? It had to come, but I'd hoped it wouldn't happen in my lifetime.

Matthew had been working in Flaky Field, and he heard the news as he came back through the village. 'If only we'd got a bit of paper,' he said, stuffing bread into his mouth. 'A bit of paper that says I've got a proper claim to this cottage and the garden.'

'You'll have a proper claim to the peppermint water

if you go on eating at that rate,' I said. 'Slow down.
We'll look for the paper after we've eaten.' But even
as I spoke I had no hope: where, in this cottage which
I'd kept properly cleaned and swept during the three
years of our marriage, could such a piece of paper be?
Had there been one I'd have found it long ago. But I
hadn't the courage to say so then. I watched Matthew
search, and at first I even helped him. 'Here, perhaps?'
I suggested, or: 'Prise out that loose brick Matthew,
perhaps your grandfather hid it there.'

'We ought to have it. We should have one. When
my father's grandfather was given leave to raise this
cottage and graze a cow and a horse he ought to have
had a bit of paper to say it was all legal and proper.'

'Perhaps he had,' I said, at last, 'but to folks that
can't read, a bit of paper mightn't be important. Perhaps your grandmother or your mother burned it.
They couldn't know that we'd ever need it.'

'That may be so,' Matthew said, slowly. 'But a piece
of paper like that—a special thing—would have to have
a special place. I don't think it was burned, I think it
was hidden. Too safely, perhaps.' He looked round the
room, then poked a knife blade behind the board that
held the coat pegs and into the spaces where the
beams had sagged. In the anxious days and nights that
followed he would suddenly leave what he was doing
as he thought of another likely hiding place. I couldn't
bear to watch: first the hope, then the despair. And I'd
say: 'Come, my dear, it's time for bed. Even if we
haven't got a paper we might get an allotment. My
mother worked in a village which was enclosed a long
time ago, and even the poorest squatter was given the
chance to rent a small-holding of land, enough to grow
some food and to keep a pig on, and they all had the
use of a common cow pasture. The landowners thought
it was a good thing—it kept down the poor rate because there weren't so many people needing parish relief. So perhaps everything'll turn out all right.' But
even as I tried to console him I thought: What if they

don't? How will we live? What will we do? I knew the answer: we would go to Sheffield to live with my aunt who kept a lodging-house. Once, on a visit, she'd hinted that she could use another pair of hands and that Matthew would be able to find work in one of the new factories there.

At last even he realized that there was no paper to give us a claim to what we'd always believed was ours, and then there was nothing but to wait while the Squire's petition went before Parliament, going about our ordinary work, watching the gooseberries swell and the pig fatten, and thinking: How long? How long shall we be able to do this?

One or two families who lived on the eastern side of the Waste had believed all along that they'd lose the rights they had thought of as theirs, and two brothers who had been in the Navy had already left to get work elsewhere. But there were those who would not think ahead to the day when the Waste would be shared out among the landowners, when they would have to bring their beasts off, when they would no longer be allowed to cut turves or take wood for their fires. 'We won't be turned off the Waste,' they said, 'stands to sense, we Franklins been here since before the Old Queen's day.' And the words 'right of ancient usage' dropped so often from their tongues that they lost their legal, bookish sound.

But on a day in June when a swollen sky rumbled with distant thunder we heard that the Squire's bill had received the Royal Assent. And later, when the Commissioners came and decided just how the land should be split up and divided among the farmers and landowners, Matthew and I and our neighbours learned just how much an old piece of paper could be worth; not having one we were to have nothing. Enclosure had come. The hunger for land had taken hold of the great open fields and the Waste—distributing them among those who could prove some ownership—with scant thought for those who had only the 'right of ancient usage'—and chopping them into neat farms with quickset and ditches and fences.

And then, as so often happens—as if people cannot accept the worst—after the despair a word was whispered and hope came again. Perhaps if we petitioned (another word now common on a cottager's lips), Squire might give us allotments, just some pasture for a cow and a piece of land where each family might grow food. It was unlikely, for the Squire was close-fisted, but we could try.

'But we gotta go about it orderly,' said Joe Parsons, whose idea it was. 'No good going along to the bailiff and just asking. We ought to see a lawyer and get him to set out the whys and wherefores.'

Money was short for everyone was hoarding against the days that were coming, but one or two of us had some small thing we could sell to raise the lawyer's fees.

And now, at this moment, the men who had been summoned to the churchyard were gathering to hear if it had been worthwhile. Small wonder that my hand on the crib was urgent, but at last Daniel's eyes had closed. I blew softly into his face but he didn't stir, so I snatched up my shawl, threw it over my shoulders and tiptoed out. Quickly I skirted the gardens and tapped at Sarah Fairchild's door. It stood ajar, for the afternoon was mild, and it creaked open under my knuckles. She was sitting by the hearth, her knees spread to hold a bowl of herbs that she was rubbing. Her broad, sleepy face looked up and quickened for a moment.

'You going to the churchyard, Hester? I *thought* you would. I said to Fairchild this morning, "Squire might've summoned the menfolk, but mark my words," I said, "Hester Calladine'll be there for sure. She'll not be left out," I said.'

'And why should I be?' I asked. 'What Sir Grenville's got to say concerns me as well as Matthew.'

'I saw him go,' she said. 'I sat by my window and saw 'em all pass.'

'Would you give an eye to Daniel while I'm gone?'

'Course I will. You should have brought him here.'

'He's sleeping. And I won't be long.'

'Then I'll go right over when I've done with these. I don't know how you darest go, though,' she said. 'Squire's bailiff did say partickerly only the men.'

'I don't see what it matters. If he's going to give us allotments then it'll all have been decided before this. And if he's not—well, what I do won't alter it.'

'But what'll Matthew say when he sees you? The only woman along a lotta men?'

'He won't see me. I'm not going into the churchyard. I'll hide at the bottom of the bank outside the wall.'

'Ah.' She sat back. There was something comfortable and smug about her plump shoulders, her round, red arms, the easy way in which she sat—something that I envied.

'You're lucky,' I said and immediately wished I hadn't spoken for I knew what was coming next; I'd heard it before, four times, and Heaven knows how many times she'd told the tale.

'I *am*,' she said. 'I can't stop marvelling over it. To think of that paper stuck down the edge of the cupboard shelf all these years, and I thought it was no more'n a wedge to hold the shelf firm. We rooted round for two days, Fairchild and me, trying to find summat, and it was sitting there all the time, covered in cobwebs and black as the devil's hearthstone. . . . There was that little old baby curl in it and a coin. Fairchild's granny must have put 'em there for safe-keeping, all wrapped up in the paper. When I saw the coin I said: "Fairchild, that's money, but it ain't what we're wanting." And he said: "Look, you great gowk, it's a dockerment—it's got writing on," and I peered and sure enough. . . . So I said: "You go straight over to Parson and get him to read it. So we got five acres and a bit more at the top end of Flaky. Course, it's a bit stony up there, and we'll have to sell some to fence the rest but—'

I nodded and smiled, and as she took breath I said quickly: 'I must go. I won't be long.'

I hurried across the Waste, picking my way over the boggy bits, holding my skirt clear of the brambles and gorse as I took the short way. Beyond the turnpike the village lay quiet, the houses clustered round the square church tower like chicks under their mother. The chestnut leaves warned the summer was over, but the day was golden as if the season were loth to leave.

In Flaky Field the gleaners had gone, and the cattle had been turned in to grope with thick, unhurried tongues for what they could find. I stopped for a moment to catch my breath and look. It was all so quiet, so unworried, unhurried, as it had been last year and the year before—as it had been for centuries. It was beautiful; I had thought it everlasting. Soon this great field, with the trodden baulks that separated one man's strip from the next would be shared out and chopped into separate farms. Soon the Waste would come under the plough.

I thrust away my sadness and crossed the turnpike, dropping down the bank at the far side, running across the glebe until I reached the church wall. Where I stood the churchyard was higher than the adjacent land, and although on the other side the wall stood only as high as my shoulder, here in the rough meadowland it towered above me. I crouched, unseen, among the brambles, noting idly a few fine berries that still hung among the thorns. Soon their ripeness would be too great to hold the core and they'd fall, black, juicy thimbles, rotten-sweet, and be taken back to the earth. It was part of the country pattern. Yet for me and for them this October afternoon would not come again.

I wriggled into a slight clearing under the wall, listening to the drone of voices on the other side, giving a name to their owners, as the same old chop-logic

that had gone on for the past year was put forward
as if it were something new.

Then there was the sound of distant hooves and I
heard Matthew say: 'Squire's coming, and look, he's
got Mr Grey with him.'

'If he needs a lawyer to prop him it don't bode too
well for us.' That was Lem Wisker.

'We put our petition in through Lawyer Grey, didn't
we? Then it's only fair and right that we get our answer through him,' said Joe Parsons. 'We paid him. Not
that I think it'll come to aught.'

The horses halted, there was a last shuffling and
scraping on the gravel, then the lawyer began to speak.
Many of his words were unfamiliar, others were spoken in too low a voice for me to hear, but I heard their
tone. I sensed and shared the hope those men held,
and felt it leave them, as Mr Grey went on. And I,
too, was emptied.

There was quiet again on the other side of the wall,
and then the muttering began. For a moment I was
afraid. Some of the men had torn the enclosure notice
from the church door during the three weeks it had
been nailed there; would someone now move forward
—just one man—and have them all clamouring and
pressing round the Squire, and then . . . ?

Then I heard Sir Grenville's voice, clear and reedy.
'The Commissioners considered all claims and did not
see fit to provide allotments, and their decision is
final. And, as Mr Grey has told you, I see little purpose. . . . There will be jobs as usual—'

'But we gotta *eat*. An' with winter wages droppin''
and no geese on the Waste—'

'Yes. What's to do wi' my cow when the Waste is
ploughed up? We can't afford to *buy* milk, and my
young un—'

'And what about my pig—with Fernwood enclosed?'

'How about the taters next year?'

'Bugger next year. What about *now*?'

The Squire spoke again, louder. 'If you'll hear me.

. . . Those who want work will find it. Fences must be raised, and there'll be wood to be hauled and split, ditches to be dug, hedges set. And farming is changing; more day labour will be needed to work the bigger farms. I can see no shortage of work for you. That is all I have to say.'

His horse scattered the gravel as he cantered away, Lawyer Grey following. A stillness had fallen on the churchyard.

'And he brought me off my diggin' just to tell me *that*,' Lem Wisker said at last.

'More fool you—diggin' someone else's land,' Joe Parsons said.

'It wa' that tiddly bit at side. I thought if I got an allotment that bit could go down to taters.'

'Oh, to hell with the allotments,' Joe Parsons answered. 'T'ain't no use blawtin' about them any more. We didn't have a chance, really, and we all knew it. If it wasn't so bloody sad it'd make you laugh. . . . Look at it: all them who had strips in the open fields come out of it with more land than they had afore 'cos they get a slice of the Waste thrown in, yet Squire don't know the difference between a barley crop and a bull's foot. An' he's hardly ever here, anyway. But *we'll* be here, quietly starving, watching our children go hungry, not even a sodding cow on the Waste to wring a drop o' milk from, no tater patch, nowhere to keep a pig. A day labourer's wages, that's all we'll have —if we're lucky. So what happens then? I'll tell you. We all fall over ourselves trying to get every little job that's going. That'll send the rate down. How much to empty a privy? To pitch a wall? Huh, you'll see. It's all happened afore in some other place.'

'Well,' put in Tommy Dobbie, mildly, 'he *did* say as there'd be work on fences and such, didn't he? Take each day as it comes, I say, and don't look too hard at the morrer.'

'You would,' Lem Wisker barked. 'But the morrer comes. Then what? Cap in hand and on the parish. I

ain't never been on the parish before, ain't never had
to look to charity for my daily bread. And another
thing, what's going to happen to our firin' I'd like to
know, wi' winter coming on, and that?'

'You heard what Squire said,' Tommy laughed. 'And
with all them fences going up I don't see much shortage of cut wood, so we must just nip out of a dark
night and up a few o' them stakes.'

Lem Wisker spat over the wall above me, and I
shrank back into the brambles. 'That's the sort o' talk
I've come to expect from you, Tommy. You don't see
no further'n your nose. You know what'll happen if
you're caught taking them fence rails. It'll be a fine of
five pound or more.'

'Well, that's what I mean,' retorted Tommy. 'I ain't
got five pounds, nor five shillin's, come to that, so I
get the wood for nothing, and they gets nothing for the
wood.'

'Talk sense, man. House of Correction—that's what
you'll get. They got you all ways.'

No word from Matthew who must still be with them.
But then, what did I expect. It had all been said before, and words were useless now. It had gone beyond
mere words.

I picked up my skirts and began to run. It would
never do for him to catch me here. It was man's business, he'd said, and nothing for me to poke my nose
into.

But it *was* my business: if there were to be no allotments, no common right of pasture, we must leave,
Matthew, Daniel and I. Oh, yes, it was indeed my
business, I thought as I hurried back across the Waste.
Matthew wouldn't be going to Sheffield alone.

TWO

If I hadn't already known the news I'd have read it on Matthew's face when he came in.

I once saw a loose bullock felled in Framley Friday market. I was only a child then, but I remember it clearly: just in that moment before it dropped, its eyes had shone with terror and surprise and pain, all rolled into one. After that I could never watch a pig-killing, although in those parts they made quite a frolic of it, with Bob Pardo scraping his fiddle and the children singing a special song and doing a funny, stiff-legged dance round the strung-up carcase. Dreading that moment when the beast's eyes looked for comfort and found none, I usually found some other place to go when there was a pig-killing.

Now Matthew's eyes had something of that look and, for all I knew, mine had, too.

I bent over the fire and stirred the cabbage and bacon. Although the pot could have seethed all day without attention, it gave me a minute to gather myself together.

'So it's Sheffield, then,' I said, as if I didn't already know. 'Well, don't look that way, Matthew. I reckon there's worse places. We half expected it, anyway. Hanging on's a sad business and if we go very soon we'll be snug and safe up there before the roads get bad. And it'll be nice to see Aunt Molly again.' (God forgive me for that lie, I thought.)

Matthew nodded, looking round the room. 'We can't take any of this stuff with us, Hester.'

'Well, I know we can't, you ninny,' I said, still in that silly, false voice. 'Come to think of it, you'd look a real comic with my granny's food hutch strapped to your back like a snail carrying its shell.'

Matthew smiled as if it hurt. "I'll get Sam Dexter along to see what he'll pay for the stuff,' I went on.

'And I'll see Bellerby about the pig and the cow.'

'No need for that,' I said, quickly. 'He's already been and spoken for them—just in case.'

I didn't see the need to tell Matthew that *I'd* walked the four miles to Bellerby's place and haggled about the price: Matthew would only think I was interfering in his business. But, as I'd intended, I did manage to wring an extra shilling out of the old skinflint. Matthew would have taken the first price offered.

When I'd first realized that we might have to leave it had seemed only sense to sell the cow and the pig before everyone else did the same and sent the price down. It's surprising how a little forethought can stretch things, but it didn't do to let Matthew know that I was just a bit sharper at looking ahead than he was.

Why, even when he asked me to marry him I'd had to speak for him, and to this day I never smell the scent of wet hawthorn blossom without remembering that evening in May. The spring rains had been heavy that year. The river had overrun its banks several times, and the land there was still very marshy. Matthew helped me across the worst parts, and sometimes if I stumbled against him I felt him tremble. I knew what was in his mind—a girl always knows—and I think he even started to say it once or twice, but he just couldn't find the words. So, one evening, when the hawthorns touched our faces with wet bloom, I held out my foot and pointed to the gaping hole in the sole of my shoe.

'These won't last another time,' I said, 'so it's an end to our walking for a while.'

Then he seemed to gather courage, and he said: 'Hester, I've wanted to ask you—'

But he stopped, so there was nothing for it but for me to whisper: 'To wed?'

He nodded, and there was such a look on his face that I wanted to weep. 'Then the answer's "yes",' I breathed.

I hadn't told him, that May evening three years ago, about the shoes I'd bespoke two weeks before and which would be ready at the cobbler's the following day. So I suppose I deceived him, but it seemed the right thing to do at the time, and I felt no guilt.

In the same way I saw no reason to reveal that I'd had a hand in settling a fair price for the beasts, so I let Matthew think that Bellerby had sought *me* out.

'I had an offer for Holly some weeks back . . .' Matthew said.

And there, I thought, I cannot interfere, for in later days, when he thinks about his horse, I don't want him to remember that I had a hand in the sale.

Anyone who buys a horse from a stranger at a fair is a fool, they said in our parts, for the chances are that the horse has been stolen or primed up, or both. And when Matthew led Holly home—led, mark, not rode—from Framley fair, I groaned inside. The creature was little more than a bag of bones, and his head drooped as if a sack of corn were slung either side of his neck. His coat was rough and dull and in places showed scurfy skin, and his ears stuck out like tiny wings. He was so ill-looking that no one had thought it worthwhile to spruce him up for the fair.

'I got him dirt cheap, Hester,' Matthew said, defiantly, jutting his chin and tightening his mouth, 'and I'm going to look for a cheap cart and do a bit of carrying.' The horse hardly looked able to pull himself along, let alone a laden cart. For three weeks Matthew just let him graze, even occasionally giving him an

apple or a crust, and the kitchen stank of the draughts
and jalap he was forever brewing. Gradually Holly
began to look a bit more like a horse. Matthew was
never-a man of words, but I reckon that creature
heard more from him than I ever did. When Matthew
spoke Holly used to turn his head sideways as if to
catch every word. So if Matthew wanted to let Holly
go cheap to a good master then it was his affair.

After he'd gone out I sat for a moment thinking, then
I stirred myself. My granny used to have a lot of say-
ings; one was 'Angels tend, herbs mend,' and another
'Rosemary eases the troubled mind'. I went over to the
chimney-shelf and shook some dried rosemary needles
into a mug and poured on hot water. After a while
the draught seemed to do its work, and I could look
about me and think clearly what must be done.

I wondered what Sam Dexter would pay for my
bits and pieces: there was my grandfather's table—
polished so that my face looked back at me as I bent
over it—and there was the food hutch and Daniel's
cradle, a chair, two stools, and my pots and dishes.
That was about all. I wouldn't get much for them. I
knew that many cottages like ours were being stripped,
some to pay fencing costs, and Sam Dexter would tell
me—probably with truth—that he had a room full of
the stuff and no one was buying them now, the new
gentry hankering after walnut and the like. Yet I
knew, too, that if I'd been *wanting* to buy a good elm
table that had been regularly waxed and polished he'd
have said no one made stuff like that now and they
were scarce as strawberries on Lady Day.

Some of the smaller things I could take with me: the
latten candlestick that had belonged to my mother and
the patchwork cushion I'd made from the scraps Mrs
Pendlebury had given me. She was one of the busiest
dressmakers in Framley, and every September, when
the trees in her garden were weighed down with fruit,
I'd go over for a couple of days and make her jams

and jellies and cordials. She always paid me a shilling and my dinner, and at the end of the second day she'd fill my bag with scraps of material—not the best, of course, she sold those—and although some of the pieces in my cushion were no bigger than your eye it was bright and pretty, the prettiest thing I had.

I'd take the skillet Mrs Craven had given me for a wedding-present. And that would be all that was left of my home. All because of enclosure.

They said it made for better farming. With a man's acres held together, all in one parcel instead of in separate strips in different parts of the open fields, and with a bit of the Waste thrown in, to boot, not many farmers and landowners wanted to stay with the old ways. I'd heard tell of a great place in Norfolk where they were marling the soil years ago to make it yield better. And then there was a place in Leicestershire where they were very particular which ram they put to which ewe to give two pounds of flesh where there'd only been one before. So it was natural, I suppose, for those who could to try better ways . . . But the poor had relied on their little piece of the Waste to keep them going when work was scarce. And even if our cows were lean and poor-looking, they did give milk. We could eat or sell our geese, the choice was ours. We had not only lost the Waste: we had lost our small dignity. But it didn't do to gnaw that bone too closely. At least, I thought, there'd be a bit of money from one thing and another—I wouldn't have liked to go to Aunt Molly's with empty pockets. And perhaps Sarah Fairchild would give me a few pence for my preserves, for she was never much good with her own.

A faint wind was scraping the leaves round the mounting-block outside the Queen's Head when we left, and it sounded like a whispered goodbye. We'd been busy during the last few days, but now with all our belongings wrapped in three blankets and Daniel closely swaddled in some of the Squire's wedding-dole linen and everything in Saxtoft done and finished with, there was time for such fancies.

I eased my foot inside my shoe against the pressure of the three shillings I'd put beneath the flannel innersole. The coins were my savings, and I hoped they'd still be there when we reached Sheffield, for I intended holding on to that bit of money come what may. It didn't make us rich, but as long as it was there we wouldn't be penniless.

Into my bodice I'd pushed a bud from the rosebush that tapped the cottage window, and I kept bending my head to catch its faint scent. When I plucked it, it had looked quite big for my sight was blurred as I shut the door for the last time. But after I'd wiped my eyes I saw it was quite tiny and brown at the edges; it would die without opening.

A few of the women and children watched us leave, and the last thing I saw before we turned out of the village was Sarah Fairchild's kerchief falling like a great, white tear.

In silence we watched the familiar things pass: the old milestone leaning askew at the roadside, Hindle Wood where I'd turned out so many of Mrs Craven's pigs to root for acorns. The oak leaves were yellowing and dropped silently on to the crushed copper bracken. Out on Flaky they were already digging holes for fenceposts, and the knock of spade on stone chimed across the fields. After we passed the northern edge of Hindle Wood the landmarks were behind us. The way ahead was new and strange, but I didn't pay it much heed: the past was still too close.

We reached Flewster as the dusk was closing down. In cottages and houses candles and dips were being lit, and the windows shone gold. I caught little snatches of life: tables ready for the evening meal, a woman dandling a child. And I thought back to Saxtoft when, sometimes at this hour, I'd gone to stand at the gate just for the pleasure of looking back towards the cottage and seeing my own golden window with the rosebush making dark threads against the light. And now in my sadness I was grateful to these unknown people in their homes. It eased me to know that, although *I* was uprooted, all through the land were homes that were lived in. And, in a strange way, I, too, was part of those people, for somewhere there was a home for me, and on some future day when the twilight came down I would sit by my window sewing or nursing Daniel, and maybe a coach would pass and a traveller, cramped and cold in the outside basket as we were now, would feel better for having seen my light.

ragged passage separated this room from another, and
through the open door I caught a glimpse of people at
supper. Two boys were rushing dishes to the tables,

THREE

I would never have thought that merely sitting all day could make the limbs shriek with weariness, but when we rattled into the yard of the Feathers where we were to stay until we took the Sheffield coach the following noon, I was relieved to hobble down, out of range at last of the sharp elbows of my neighbour, for we'd been rattled together like a pair of dice.

After Matthew had paid the landlord's wife for our night's lodging we were taken up to a room in the roof. The only window was a tiny square set high in the gable, dark against the whitened walls. The room was very small and so low that we couldn't stand upright on one side, but it was fairly clean, and at least it was too small to allow sharing: I disliked the thought of lying with strangers who might be drunkards, thieves or worse.

Daniel, fretful and sleepy, wriggled in my arms, jutting his chin as Matthew so often did. I sank down on the mattress, guided his mouth to my breast, and he quietened, as if he drew from me some of the gloom of the day. I nursed him until he slept, then I put him down, covered him and stole downstairs to join Matthew.

I took a seat on the bench opposite him and looked about me. We were in a small, low room with a well-sanded floor and a bright fire burning on the hearth. A flagged passage separated this room from another, and through the open doors I caught a glimpse of people at supper. Two boys were rushing dishes to the tables, and a plump woman followed carrying a steaming tureen. The smell of herrings, apples, hare cooking with onions nudged my hunger, and I set out the bacon pasties and two apples and a few nuts which I'd brought.

With the fire warming my back and the easing of my aching limbs, and the food I'd eaten, I must have dozed, for I was jerked awake by a voice saying: 'You'll forgive me, but I wonder if you would spare me a little of your time.'

I looked up to see a tall man standing by the table. I flicked Matthew a warning glance: we'd heard of the men who made their livings off travellers such as we. If they weren't rough and brutish and frightening they had tongues like sweet oil; either way they'd have your money before they were done.

The stranger smiled at our hesitation. 'The matter is urgent,' he said, gently, 'otherwise I would not have disturbed what is obviously a much needed rest.'

Matthew rose. 'Sit down, then, sir, for I'm sure our time is of little matter for the next day or so.'

I was satisfied to see that the man sat on Matthew's right. The linen purse was in Matthew's left pocket, and with the greatest skill in the world this man couldn't have got his fingers on it. I sat back, watching him.

He had a good face with a long, curly mouth, and although he was simply dressed his clothes had a look of quality, from the mouse-coloured breeches to the plain linen neck-cloth. His boots, too, though creased with wear in their lacquered folds, had not been shaped on some village last.

'I was about to go to my room,' he began, 'when I saw you, and I believe you might be able to help me.'

'A beggar,' I thought, but not believing it.

As if I'd spoken aloud the man said: 'I want only a few minutes of your time, and it will not be wasted. You're leaving your home because of enclosure? Am I not right?'

Matthew nodded.

'And you're going north to find work?'

'To Sheffield,' Matthew said.

'Ah. Well, I am preparing a paper listing some of the evils of enclosure, suggesting possible ameliorations. If I can get it into the right hands within the next week or two I have great hopes that it may eventually help others in similar cases. You will appreciate, then, that the matter is pressing, for the more information I can get the greater import it will carry. Of course,' he smiled, ruefully, 'I know that any good it will do comes too late for you . . .' He sat looking at us for a moment. 'But I'd suggest the matter could be more agreeably conducted over a little refreshment. Boy,' he called, rapping on the table, 'bring two glasses of brandy and a Madeira for the lady.' To me he said: 'I trust you're partial to Madeira, madam?'

'Oh, yes indeed,' I said, although I'd never tasted it.

'I've seen many such as you on my travels,' he continued, as the drinks were put before us. 'Somehow one recognizes them. There is a look . . . a likeness. And you're going to Sheffield, you say?'

Matthew nodded quickly and coughed over the brandy.

'I have an uncle there,' the man said, thoughtfully. 'He has a wheelwright's business. Perhaps if I were to give you a letter of introduction he may be able to be of help. My name, by the way, is Morland. Henry Morland.'

'That would be very kind,' I said, 'I mean if you were to give us a letter—'

'Then, in return, perhaps you'll answer a few questions,' he said to Matthew.

I sat back and flicked a few crumbs from my skirt and fluffed out the little grey shawl; I didn't want it written in Mr Morland's paper that Hester Calladine was a draggle-tail.

I sat idly watching the man's hands curled round the stem of his glass. They were small and smooth, like a

lady's. I couldn't take my eyes off them as they rested,
seemingly boneless, like a pale snake coiled.

I looked at the man's face. He was watching me, and
he smiled. I turned away, my face suddenly hot. 'I'm
bosky already,' I thought, 'after only two sips.'

'Now tell me,' Mr Morland said to Matthew, 'where
are you from?'

'Saxtoft,' Matthew said, and as if the name unrolled
the boulder that dams a stream it all poured out in the
longest speech I'd ever heard him make. 'And that's
how it was,' he finished. 'All my family for generations past worked that land and lived in that cottage.
But, you see, there was no paper to say it was ours.'
He gulped the last of his brandy.

Mr Morland nodded. 'I've seen it all before, although
that can be of little comfort to you.' He caught the arm
of the passing boy. 'Bring the same,' he said, then
turned to me. 'I trust the Madeira is to your liking?'

'It's most pleasant, sir.'

'Sad as your story is,' he said, earnestly, 'I presume
you're not entirely without means now that you've sold
everything?'

As if a few coins could make up for it! I decided it
was time I had his ear. Enclosure had affected me as
well as Matthew. So I told him everything in a tumble
of words: about Sam Dexter's miserable price for my
furniture, about my nice little job making jams for
Mrs Pendlebury, about my little garden and the pink
rose beneath the window. And it all came back—the
sadness, the leaving, and I wished, wheelwright uncle
or no, the man had never come to sit with us.

Matthew was scowling at me, and I knew I'd been
talking long enough. So I said: 'No, sir, we're *not* without means. But one day you have all you need for living, and the next it's as if everything had shrunk to fit
only one pocket.' I realized, shocked, that tears were
knotting my throat.

'The Bible says: "Lay not up for yourselves treasures
upon earth—"'

' "Where moth and rust doth corrupt, and where thieves break through and steal," ' I finished. 'Are you a preacher?' The man smiled and shook his head. 'Well,' I went on, ignoring Matthew's out-thrust chin, 'the Bible says all kinds of things. There's a saying for everything, and some of them don't tally at all. So you must simply pick out the ones that fit best. Take old Amos Simmons—*you* remember him, Matthew. He lived in Saxtoft,' I explained to Mr Morland, 'and when things went wrong he'd say: "The Lord giveth, and the Lord taketh away. Blessed be the name of the Lord." And whilst he sat there by his chimney waiting for something else to be taken away, his wife went about doing a man's work to feed them all. I often thought it should have been: "Blessed be the name of Elizabeth Simmons".'

I shook off Matthew's foot which had caught me a sharp kick. 'And all I know is this: that cottage was our home, and it seemed that whatever went into it, and into my life, would be put there by—*these*.' I held out my two hands.

Morland's eyes were twinkling and his mouth quirking, but he only said: 'Your feeling is understandable, and you have my heartiest sympathy. But you must have faith. All this may be working for good. Have you thought of that? Tomorrow I shall give you a letter to my uncle and, after that, who knows? You're young. You're both in good health. You won't go under. Your spirit, Madam, will ensure that.' He gave me a mocking smile in which I saw a certain amused admiration. I felt my face and neck grow hot again. 'And now, I know you will be wanting to retire, so a small drink before we go up, perhaps?'

The anger left me suddenly, and I felt tired, so tired. This morning and the pink rose seemed years away. My limbs felt heavy, and the warmth from the fire and the lamps, the smoke, the food smells wove a blanket around me whilst the Madeira spread a sleepy glow within me. I felt as I had, sometimes, in the past, when, after a busy day, I'd sit by the fire to catch up with myself and for a few minutes let my mind float away.

Mr Morland's voice roused me. 'As I told you, I am no preacher, and although Madam has scant respect for some of the lessons laid down for our guidance, I should like to suggest that we go to your room and, in quietness, pray together for a moment.'

I drifted towards the stairs, and my feet seemed a long way from my legs. At the foot the man stood aside to let me, then Matthew, pass.

Upstairs I lit the stub of candle and we all knelt.

'Lord be watchful over thy children,' Mr Morland said. 'Guide their steps through the coming days, and bring them into the land of milk and honey. Keep thy light before them so that they may see the way of thine abiding love. Amen.'

'Amen,' I said, my voice sounding loud. I stayed there on my knees as he closed the door behind him. The land of milk and honey . . . The preacher at Saxtoft had spoken of it, and I always pictured a green meadow much, much bigger than Flaky, with cows knee-deep in lush grass, and an orchard beyond with a row of bee skeps. Perhaps God—this man's god (and, after all, he was an educated man so he should have more idea about God than I)—was not that angry, red face above a curling white beard who called pleasure 'sin' and exacted full payment. Perhaps God was like the picture of the boy Jesus that had hung in Mrs. Craven's bedroom—just a boy cradling a lamb, with such a look of love about him . . . The land of milk and honey . . . Could Sheffield be that, even though I knew it must be different from my mind's green picture? As I knelt there with the candle-light gently flickering and the Madeira working its sweet ease within me, it seemed that it could.

I was awake soon after dawn, and after I had fed Daniel I lay watching the sky lighten beyond the tiny

window. This morning I was happy. Maybe the pray-
ers had helped. And there was the letter Mr Morland
would give us. Perhaps I'd spoken up too sharply
the night before—my tongue had caused me trouble in
the past—but yesterday had been a bad day, and the
wine had loosed my thoughts.

The sky grew pale. There was the noise of hooves
and voices in the yard below. The town was waking.
I'd never been in Flewster before, and most likely I'd
never be here again; there was a market today, and I
might as well see it. I stood up on the mattress and
reached for my comb from Matthew's jacket pocket.

Then I was dashed awake, all thought of a pleasant
morning gone. I bent and shook Matthew roughly,
hardly waiting for him to grunt before I burst out: 'The
money. Where did you put the money?'

'Eh? Oh—in my pocket.'

'No. No. It isn't there.'

I dropped back on to the mattress. I remembered
those smooth serpent hands. 'That fine God-watch-
you fellow has picked your pocket,' I said. 'It must
have been when he followed you upstairs.'

Matthew was fully awake now, running his hands
through his dark, tousled hair, squinting his blue eyes
against the light.

'No,' he said, dully. 'The money was there when I
hung up the coat.'

'Then why didn't you—' I burst out, then stopped.
I had been going to say: "Why didn't you tuck it into
your shirt or hide it under the mattress?"—things I
would have done. But Matthew didn't think like me.
And anyway, would I, tipsy as I had been, have given
a thought to it?

'Then somebody's been in and robbed us,' I said.

We both sat quietly, shocked. Then Matthew said:
'Mr Morland'll help us. It's a good thing we ran into
him. I'll go and find him now and explain. He'll help.'

I sat like a stone until he came back, and when I
saw his face I knew.

'He's gone, Hester. He told the landlord he'd a long ride today, and he left before dawn. And his name wasn't Morland. He'll be miles away by now.'

'With our money. So he *was* a serpent—'

'What do you mean?'

'All that talk,' I said, 'the praying and the letter to the uncle. The brandy and Madeira—don't you see? They were to make us sleep. And coming up here to pray—oh, can't you *see*, Matthew, just so's he could spy out the room and see where we would lie and where we would be likely to put our clothes. I *knew* there was something false—'

'Well if you knew why didn't you say—'

'How could I? And you tell me I'm fanciful. It might have been just fancy . . . He *seemed* kind; he had a good face, and gentlemen *do* write papers about enclosure and slaves and—But, somehow, there was something not *right*. I know,' I said, suddenly, 'didn't he say: "I trust you're partial to Madeira, Madam?" Now why should he ask that? If, as he said, he knew we were just ordinary country folk, then he must have known I'd never have tasted Madeira. Oh, what a jenny-ass I was.'

Matthew sat frowning, cracking his knuckles. 'What are we going to do now, Hester?'

'Our home and the pig. And your Holly, Matthew—all for three brandies and three Madeiras. A mess of pottage.' I began to laugh shrilly. 'At least we got that much for the sale of everything we had.'

'Don't. Stop it, Hester.'

I felt the ragged laughter die in my throat. I stood looking at Matthew's bent head, his hands hanging slackly between his knees. I knelt down beside him. 'We've still got each other,' I said.

'Yes.' From his tone it seemed as if he didn't much care.

I made an effort. 'Look, Matthew, we've lost our money, and no amount of sitting waiting is going to bring it back. And you ask what we're going to do.

Well, we're going to Aunt Molly's, the same as we were yesterday. This way it'll take a little more time, that's the only difference. And look—I have this.'

I slipped off my shoe and lifted the flannel shape I'd made to line it more warmly, and I took out the three shillings.

'I saved this before we were married. I thought if I didn't take to your ways I'd put a few miles between us.' I spoke banteringly, trying to wheedle a smile from his bitter mouth, but his face didn't change. 'It meant something else, too. It meant that, no matter how bad things got, we'd never be pauper-poor. It made me feel . . . safe.'

Matthew still didn't speak.

'Well,' I said, at last, 'it's come in useful, hasn't it? Because *this* is the bad time, now.'

I took his hand and folded his fingers over the money, and a strange, shamed look as if I'd un-covered something best left hidden passed over his face. And as we picked up our bundles and left the room I thought sadly how much better it would have been for both of us if Matthew could have been the one to bring out the coins, the one to say: 'See, we're not poor, for I've saved this.'

FOUR

In Flewster market-place the stalls were set up, and a few women pressed round the crockery to get the pick of the day's bargains. Without a backward glance I followed Matthew, threading our way through the mist which hung, thin as watered milk, between the buildings. Beyond the archway on one side of the square a street ran northwards, and pinned to the grey stone wall of the last house a rose bush sprayed its late red blooms. One of them, open-hearted, brought to mind the red rose my mother had sewn from a few scraps of velvet, and which she wore pinned to her dress whenever she went out.

I've been told I looked like my mother, being thin and dark and straight-backed, and I was secretly pleased. But whatever I am she was more so. She had a fine, rather stern face: stern that is until she smiled, and then her cheeks lifted, tilting her eyes, and lifting the years from her face, too. Her teeth were good to the day she died, and she cared for them with a scrap of coarse linen and salt. When someone said I smiled like her, I looked for no greater compliment.

When we went visiting as we sometimes did in the afternoons when I was a child, even if it were only to a cottage across the green, she dressed her hair carefully and wore the shabby little rose. And as I grew older and knew moments of discontent and disappointment, I'd play a secret game which I called 'borrowing Mother's eyes'—for she saw beauty in a toad, wonder in a weed. It seemed to me that her life with my father was joyless, but to her it was enough to be alive, and despite so much that could have made her a miserable, cowed creature she was, I think, the happiest woman I ever knew. She had the gift of taking up life with both hands as if it were a prize. I was thinking of her as we left Flewster and the gardens gave way to fields.

How would Mother have felt if all her money had been stolen, and she had seventy miles or more to trudge? One thing was sure, she wouldn't be going along mumpishly as I was. She'd be stepping out with a brave straight back and a ready smile. The limp red rose would be bobbing at her neck. Well, I hadn't got a velvet rose at my front, but I had my small son strapped to my back. *She* would have found joy in him—a gift to carry, not a burden to bow the shoulders. And, as always, the thought of Mother heartened me, and in spite of everything I suddenly felt that it was good to be walking through the fresh, floating mist—indeed, it was far better than being thrown about in the basket behind the coach.

The dew had knotted with crystal the webs that laced the hedgerows and the tangle of old man's beard, and the berries of the bittersweet sparkled, red and glassy. Then the mist lifted, and it was like plucking off the dust-sheets from the furniture in Mrs. Craven's spare room. All the colours and shapes of the land stood clear: the rusting seed spikes of the dock, the gold-rimmed birch leaves, the greens and coppers, and the warm brown of ploughed land reaching to the brow of a hill and losing itself in a wine-coloured haze of saplings. The day grew warm, the sky was high and blue, and the earth dozed gently towards its winter sleep.

'It's lovely, isn't it?' I said to Matthew. 'I'm *glad* I'm not riding the basket today. I feared I'd cracked a rib yesterday—all that jolting.' I was half laughing, hoping to cheer him. But he was still sunk in gloom, his eyebrows one continuous line, his eyes on the ground before him. I looked at his brown knuckles clenching the cords of the bundles he carried, and had my hand been free I'd have touched him, but he strode on ahead of me, only turning when I spoke.

Poor Matthew; doubtless he was thinking of Holly, of the loss of our home and our money; perhaps he felt ashamed, blaming himself for the state we'd been brought to. So I tried to think of things to say that would cheer him. I knew that if I likened the mists to Mrs Craven's dust-sheets he would tell me I was being fanciful—he was always telling me that—so I spoke of everyday things: see that snug farm, what a dust this gig's raising, perhaps we might get a lift into the next town. But Matthew only grunted.

Daniel rode my back quietly, and I made up a little song:

> My son Daniel,
> When he's a man he will
> Ride a horse, trot, TROT

I'd bounce him on the last 'trot' and his fat, deep chuckle set me laughing. When I stopped to feed him his small fists kneaded my breast, while his eyes stared at me unwinking, serious, as if to say: 'This is important. This is my food. *You* are my food.' I delighted in those moments, despite Matthew's gloominess.

That night we stopped at an inn and shared an outside loft with decent folk, like ourselves going north to find work.

The following morning had a drift of dampness about it, and later the wind swung to the west and the rain began, soaking my cloak until it hung cold and heavy and cumbersome. I was holding Daniel within its folds, and the unwieldly bundle I carried in my other hand made walking awkward. At last we took shelter in a barn; the farmer's wife said we could stay the night, and she dried our clothes for us. We'd done little more than four miles that day.

We went on through the rain of the next day. The rutted roads were now boggy, and my shoes which had been dried too quickly were baked into hard ridges that chafed and broke the skin. I took them off and tucked them into my bundle.

'Now I really do look like some poor creature of the roads,' I said to Matthew. 'Thank God Sarah Fairchild can't see me now.' I laughed, ruefully.

'What? Yes. We're in a poor state. And to think . . . Perhaps we should have stayed in Saxtoft and made the best of it. I could've got work on the fencing for a bit—'

'But we *talked* about it, Matthew. The work wouldn't have lasted. And *we'll* get to Sheffield. We'll get there and forget all about this.' He only shrugged, and after that I couldn't think of anything to say.

When a blue gig came spanking by I leaped out of its path and half fell into a ditch, grabbing for a brake to steady myself, and almost throwing Daniel into the thorns. He was badly scratched about the face and set up a great wailing. We must have looked a sorry sight for, at the next village, the children jeered and tried to set the dogs on us.

It should have been a simple thing to rest, to collect a few of the driest twigs and start a fire, to spread a blanket over a low-growing bough for shelter, but our appearance was against us. We were vagrants who might take the precious winter fuel, who might steal a chicken or poach a rabbit, who might—God forbid— fall ill or break a limb or deliver a child, and so throw the burden of our being on the parish rates until they could send us back to Saxtoft—penniless and dirty to the village we'd left with sadness. I could almost see Sarah Fairchild's broad, red face and hear her gloating pity. No! We could *not* go back!

So we kept on, sheltering at night in the lee of a

hedge or by a rocky outcrop, and drinking stream water muddy from the rains. Days and nights followed each other namelessly. I forgot all but the sodden weight of my clothes, the shivering chill and then the burning the throbbing ache of my feet and the burden of Daniel, now fretful with hunger, for what I'd silently feared now seemed to be happening. I was no longer able to feed him properly.

I tried then, oh, how I tried, to call back Mother, to see the brave red rose. But they were distant things belonging to another more comfortable life. Every hour or two I'd try to rouse myself. 'Damn it to hell,' I'd think, gritting my teeth against the prick of pebbles buried in the mud, 'stiffen yourself, girl. In a few days it will all be done. Keep walking, keep going. This foot now, and now this. It's got to end sometime.' And for a while I'd go forward firmly, but only for a while.

Then, strangely, I began to think about tea. And I couldn't lose the thought. I tormented myself fancying its dry scent rising on the steam, the warmth in a fat, brown pot, the warmth in a parched throat, in a shivering chest and belly. I thought of the rare times when I'd drunk tea in Mrs Craven's kitchen, or, even more occasionally, with my mother. Then I stopped thinking. I only felt. Tired. Sleep—I wanted to sleep. In the wet I wanted to lie down and never get up again. I was tired to the very marrow.

It was late afternoon, and that day the darkness did not really lift but hung in the sky as if waiting for night. We still had a long way to go: two or three more days. Was there ever a time when I wasn't walking? I felt as if I'd been walking all my life, only now it was more of a slow ooze that carried me forward. The 'me' was the shape trapped between the hot, throbbing lumps that felt every tiny stone, and the bobbing, burning, muzzy thing plastered with wet hair. Somewhere fastened to me was a tick, Daniel, moaning and making hopeless sucking noises.

When I stopped to try and nurse him I'd stir myself, holding him close, seeking to tie us both in a thread of comfort. 'We'll soon be there, my lamb, warm and snug, and it will all be over. There'll be warm milk for you there.' But I *knew* we'd never reach Aunt Molly's, and I'd weep a little then, and fall into nearsleep until Matthew shook me.

The rain was pocking the river as we came to a little stone bridge. Matthew, a few paces ahead, plodded across. He set his bundles on the ledge and waited. I was bedraggled and done, bent against the ache in my side and the weight of Daniel's head flopping on my shoulder.

Matthew turned, stared at me for a moment, then came back. He peered into my face, and he took Daniel. He threw my bundle into the hedge bottom.

'We'll get that later,' he said in a voice that came from far away. 'There's a hut or something on the far side. We're going to get dry and rest there if I have to knock someone down for it.'

And now I was beyond caring. I could have gone on and on in the same dull motions, or I could rest. No matter, for nothing could put out the fire in my feet or smooth the cramp from my side, or make any difference to the certainty that inside this dirty, tired body a small new life was growing.

FIVE

If I'd had my wits about me when Matthew half carried me into the hut I'd have noticed several things which later puzzled me, but, spent as I was, I just let him help me down to the earth floor, and for a time I knew no more.

Then he was shaking me awake, and the flames dancing on the broken hearthstone lit the yellow mug of milk he held out. I saw beyond the door which sagged from one leather strap that outside it was almost dark. I hitched myself upright and leaned my back against the wall while I tore a strip from my kerchief, dipped it into the milk and dribbled a little into Daniel's whimpering mouth. I was still not fully awake, but gradually the sense of Matthew's words cut into my numbness.

'It's all right, Hester. We can stay until you're properly rested. And I've got work tonight at the inn. Seems one of the maids poisoned her hand, so I'm helping out. I've got to go now, but I've made you a good fire, and you'll be all right here.' He threw more wood on to the flames from the small heap in the corner, then he disappeared into the dark.

I sat for a while, feeling the warmth come back to me. The drop of milk I'd taken had eased my throat, and now I was beginning to notice things about the hut. It was almost crumbling, yet I could see that the walls had recently been patched, and the rough thatch must have been tight for it was quite dry inside. Bracken and sticks lay in a heap in a corner, and on its side on the hearth lay a lidless kettle, chained by its handle to a staple in one of the chimney bricks. I wondered idly who lived here, and—supposing someone did—why had they never bothered to hang the door properly. Or perhaps they'd recently died, I thought, and soon the place would rot into the earth. Or could it be that, despite Matthew's assurance, someone would come in soon and order me out. But for the moment it was enough to *be* there, resting, gradually warming, able to drip the thin skimmed milk into Daniel's funnelled mouth and stop his whimpering. At last he slept, so I took off my cloak and spread it near the hearth to dry, ran my fingers through my hair, then I, too, slept.

I was wakened by a rustling noise and a draught of cold air.

'Matthew?' I said, fearfully, struggling up.

'What's that?' a sharp voice asked.

'Who *is* it?' I was afraid now.

''Tis Nancy. I saw the glimmer o' light through the doorway, and I thought mebbe you'd let me share your fire. I'm parched for a drink.'

I moved my cloak aside and threw more sticks onto the dying fire. The woman—Nancy—came in and squatted by the hearth. She poured some ale from a bottle into the kettle, then, as the flames leapt, set it on the fire. 'You'll have a sup with me, lass?'

'Thank you.' I could smell the ale, and weak though it might be it teased the warm moisture into my mouth. As the flames took hold I saw her more clearly: a tall, gaunt figure, her face scored by a thousand wrinkles and seams, like a walnut, and of the same colour.

I untied my bundle and brought out the heel of a loaf and a knob of cheese. They were both hard and dry, but I'd held on to them much as I'd held on to my shillings, although they were now gone, against the moment when we *must* eat or starve, and I'd gone on telling myself that, thank God, we hadn't quite reached that state yet. Anyway, I had wanted to keep the food until our next meal was certain. Now, however, I hacked a slice from the bread and speared it with my knife, holding it to the flames. Then I sliced the cheese on to the bread. I laid my skillet across the fire until it was really hot then I held it over the cheese. It softened and filled the the hut with a mouth-watering smell. I cut the bread into two pieces and handed one to the woman. She poured the ale into a brown mug and set it between us. All in silence. Did ever smoky bread and stale cheese and weak ale taste so well.

Afterwards she loosened her skirt, belched and sat back. 'That were champion,' she said, holding out her hands to the flames, then rubbing them together with a sound like rustling leaves. 'I were clemmed.' Then she turned to look at me. 'And what brings you to Stoke Friary?'

'Is that the name . . . ? We're on our way to Sheffield,' I said.

'Then you've got a fair step to go. Just you and the bain?'

'No, my husband, too. He's working in the inn to-night.'

'That'll be the Green Man—George Rowson's place. Well, he'll not do too badly there. You don't look in much fettle to be going to Sheffield, though. You'd do better to stop and rest a bit.'

'Who lives in this hut?' I asked.

'No one. It's stood empty for nigh on three years now.'

'But the walls have been patched. And why hasn't the roof fallen in?'

'Squire keeps it like this.' She laughed, showing toothless gums. 'It's one of his notions—or Miss Olivia's I shouldn't wonder. It's this way: the Squire's a good man. Kind, see? There's gentry and there's gentry, if you take my meaning. An' he keeps it like this—*just* like this—for anyone on the road who might

have need of it. If it was all done up pretty and proper
you wouldn't have stopped, would you? No, you'd
have thought someone lived here. And if Squire didn't
do anything at all to it, then, like you said, the roof
would have fallen in, and it'd be no good to no one.
This way, he thinks, is just about right to keep a body
dry and warm. Mind, you can't stay more'n a few days.
You can't squat long; it's for anyone who might need
it, see.'

'Well, we won't be here long,' I said, wryly. 'We've
got to move on as quickly as we can.'

She was quiet for a moment, then: 'Course, it's not
for me to say, but walking's all right for some . . . like
me. I've always walked. Born on the road, I was, and
I know 'em like the veins on my hand. But you—'

'We set out by coach, in the basket,' I explained.
'But our money was stolen.'

'Ah. Well, why don't you stay here just a few days.
It looks like you could do with it. I've just come up
from the village—I got some regular calls there, and I
heard that Squire's setting on men at the gravel hole.
Having a new drive made up at the Old Hall. Happen
your man could get work there for a day or so.'

'But would they take . . . a stranger?'

She shrugged. 'Not for me to say just who they'll
set on, but they're in a bit of a hurry to get that drive
sprinkled—some ball or other I shouldn't wonder—and
Squire's not one to deny a willing man work. If he'll
dig I should think he'll do.'

The word 'squire' brought to me a picture of Sir
Grenville in Saxtoft who didn't care a peppercorn for
any of the people. But here was a different kind of
squire who would give a stranger work and who would
keep a hut in shape enough just so that poor straws
like us could have a dry bed.

'I'd planned on staying the night here,' Nancy said.
'I thought it'd be empty.'

'There's room for all of us,' I said.

'Thanks. I'm off towards Bath tomorrow; I peddle a

few things.' She pulled out of her bundle a neat roll of canvas and unlaced it to reveal hundreds of little pockets, each stuffed with thread, needles, scraps of ribbon, combs and such. 'I sometimes think a hearth of my own is what I need at my age, but truth to tell I've never known a settled life, and mebbe it's too late for me to start now. Course, when I had Joe along with me it was different. We had a little cart then, and a donkey, and we carried more stuff, and Joe was handy and did a bit of tinkering along the way. Then he took ill and died, near Chester, it was, then the donkey died, so I sold the cart and now I walk. But I tire easy these days. Still—I've never stayed overlong in one place, and I reckon I'm too old to start now. So I just keep going. Well, I think I'll catch a nap.'

She wore a bonnet known as a calash, then very fashionable, shaped on hoops big enough to cover without crushing the high hair-dressing of the day. On Nancy's bonnet the hoops were broken, and her scanty hair did nothing to fill it. Her face looked like a little brown animal peering from a dark hole.

'You're admiring my hat,' she said proudly, as she pulled the strings and it collapsed round her neck. 'It was given to me by one of my ladies. I pick up quite a bit as I travel.' She took off her ragged brown cloak, turned it inside out, rolled herself in it and was soon snoring gently. I sat nursing Daniel until Matthew came. He brought two little mutton pies and made me eat both.

'I got my food at the inn,' he said, 'and Mr Rowson says I can go back tomorrow and saw some logs.' He put an arm round me. 'You feeling better, Hester? You look it. I was a bit scared when I saw you this afternoon—you looked bad. You should have said—I didn't know.'

'I'm much better,' I whispered nodding over towards Nancy. 'We've got a visitor, and she tells me they're taking on men at the gravel hole.'

'Do you think I—'

'She said there's a chance.'

'Then, soon as I've finished at the inn tomorrow I'll go and see. It's been grand to work again,' he said, 'even if it was only slicing carrots in a kitchen . . . women's work.'

Matthew had gone when I awoke the next morning. The kettle was humming on the fire, and Nancy and I shared the last of the bread and cheese. When I picked up Daniel to give him the rest of the milk, she said: 'Let me do it. I never had a bain. Seemed I was a fruit that wouldn't ripen. Mebbe if I'd had one I could have made my home with him now—just for the bad months.' She sat trickling the milk into Daniel's mouth, her face soft and dreaming.

Later she opened the door and sniffed the air, wrinkling her nose like a hound. 'Set fair for a bit,' she said, 'so I'll get on my way. What's your name, lass? Hester Calladine—that's a grand-sounding name. Mine's Nancy Roydhouse—real Yorkshire, that one. Well, next time I get up to Sheffield I'll keep an eye open for you. Not that there's much chance of seeing you, but stranger things've happened. But do as I bid, stay here as long as it takes to scrape a few pence together and get yourself right.'

I stood in the doorway and watched her cross the stone bridge, going the way we had come yesterday. She turned at the end, and I waved, then she was hidden by the trees.

My head was still a bit woolly, but I set about putting myself to rights. I made several journeys to the river with my skillet, then I heated the water in the kettle. I hung a blanket over the doorway and washed myself and Daniel. I cleaned up my blue dress and mended the rents with the needle and some of the soiled thread that Nancy had given me.

Sunshine was flooding the tiny room, dulling the red fire. My spirits climbed. Daniel lay watching a few flies basking in a sunlit patch on the wall. He was quiet now, and there was a little colour in his cheeks.

I made a poultice of the few dock leaves I had been able to find, bound the green mess round my feet with more strips torn from my kerchief, and I squeezed into my shoes. All this took time, for I had to rest often, but at last I felt clean and half-way respectable and refreshed. It was time, I thought, to take a look at this village of Stoke Friary.

Ahead lay the river, glinting in the cold sunlight and looping away behind a spinney that rose on the far bank. Running the same way as the river, but sep- arated from it by meadowland, was the road, and further along, on my right, a few cottages faced south- wards to the river. I walked slowly, looking at the neat, winter-tidy gardens, the potato garths, the fowls that pecked under the hedges. Where the cottages were set side-by-side slabs of stone made a raised path along their fronts. I turned the corner by the row of almshouses and reached the inn and stood looking through the archway into the yard. Matthew came from an outbuilding dragging some small logs tied up with rope. He waved and called that he'd soon be done, and he'd bring more milk for Daniel. I nodded and made to move on when a woman came from an- other of the outhouses, saw me and stopped. Then she said: 'If you want to come inside and warm yourself until he's done you can.'

And after that things happened quickly, willy-nilly, like knocking over one skittle that touches another, sets it rocking, and that one, in turn, nudges another until, all along the line, they fall.

The first thing happened while I was sitting in the bright warm inn kitchen. I noticed the woman, Mrs Rowson, looking at my dress, and I pulled the skirts round me, ashamed, for I hadn't managed to wash away all the dirt and I knew that I must still look a draggle-tail. But she was looking at my mending which

I'd done with care. She asked if I'd like to do some plain sewing for her. It seemed that a new turnpike road was to run behind the village, and she had hopes of letting two or three of the upstairs rooms to travellers. She'd bought bolts of stuff for sheets, but she was a poor hand at sewing. 'And you know the way it is,' she added, 'you need to have a good long run at a sheet hem, and I'm always needed somewhere else.'

So I had a job, a good job in the warm, with my dinner given to me and even a cup of tea, for Mrs Rowson said that no day was right without one brewing. She baked a marrow bone, cracked it and spread a little of the meat on a crust, and that kept Daniel quiet for a while.

By noon Matthew had finished the sawing and had gone along to the far end of the village to the gravel hole, and as he hadn't returned I supposed they'd set him on. If we could keep this up for a few days, I thought, as I threaded my needle, we may be able to pay for a wagon ride into Sheffield.

Then the second skittle wobbled and fell: whilst Matthew was working at the gravel hole the man who drove the cart they were loading mentioned that one of the Squire's carriage horses was sick.

Now Matthew's neat-handed with beasts. As a boy he'd watched his grandfather treat sick animals for, being a farrier, the old man had come to know a bit about such things. Also, his eldest daughter, Matthew's aunt, had at one time gone off with the gypsies (which hadn't pleased the old man one bit), but when her husband died she came home, bringing with her stories of their ways with horses. And, as well, as there are the little bits of learning that get passed down, father to son: some swear that a rowan sprig will keep a horse healthy, others hang up a stone with a hole in it outside the stable to keep away the night-witches, for there were tales that they rode the horses at midnight, bringing them back only when they were blown. A lot of this might be just old say-so, but somehow these stories stick, perhaps because there's often a grain of sense to them. Anyway, one way and another, Matthew had a way with horses.

One of the things which Matthew's grandfather used to clear a wound was mouldy bread. He always had a few damp dishes standing about and a crust or two growing a green coat. None of us could see how it worked, and I secretly thought that if I had a bit of mucky bread strapped to me then I'd *make* myself get better just to be rid of it. Perhaps the beasts felt that way, too. I knew that was nonsense, of course. But then so was thinking that the green fuzz healed. Yet it did. It had worked with Holly, so I stopped trying to figure it out.

The Squire's man gave Matthew a ride up to the stables to look at this horse. The head groom, Hoskett, stared at Matthew a bit high-nosed for they'd already tried everything. And Matthew, hearing this, could only come up with the idea of the mould: if it cured things outside, he said, then mightn't it do the same for the inside? At last the groom tipped his bullycock, scratched his head, then said: 'Well it's kill or cure, so do your best,' and he sent Jobey, the stable-boy, off to find anything mouldy he could lay his hands on.

This gave Matthew a chance to look round the stables, and there was one horse that particularly took his eye.

'Saladin, his name is,' Matthew said, when he was telling me all this. 'The squire's not had him long. He's tall, Hester, he stands higher than any horse I've ever seen, and his coat's like wet pitch. Real high-bred and nervous, but he didn't seem to mind me.'

After that Matthew went up to the stables every day to look at the sick horse (and, I suspect, the big, black one) and gradually the sick one picked up a bit, though whether or not it was due to the mould I never knew.

On the following Monday the last load of gravel had been lifted, and I'd almost finished Mrs Rowson's sheets. It was all very timely for they would be done and ironed and put away on the Tuesday, and the carrier would be calling on Wednesday on his way up to Sheffield. Mrs Rowson said that if we waited until then he might give us a ride in, so that we shouldn't arrive in Sheffield with empty pockets after all. Although we hadn't earned much I had hated the thought of going to Aunt Molly's without the price of a bed, for I remembered her as close-fisted and ungiving.

My feet were almost healed, and Daniel was taking milk from a mug fairly well and cutting his teeth on anything he could find or was given. Our stay in Stoke Friary had been happy, and I was sorry to be leaving this trim little village where people had been good to us.

On Tuesday Mrs Rowson paid me and gave me a piece of bacon and some oatcakes for our evening meal. It was late afternoon and when I got back to the hut the fire was dead. There were no sticks, and I guessed Matthew had gone to find some. It was almost dark when he finally came. He was so breathless that at first I couldn't get any sense from him, but when I'd put the kettle on, and he'd calmed himself a bit, he told me that he had been in the spinney getting sticks when he'd heard a noise.

'Hooves,' he said, 'and something else—a sort of rushing rustling sound, so I dodged out of sight behind some trees. Then I saw them: Saladin going like Jack Shock . . . dragging—well—I guessed it was the Squire. Without thinking I jumped out and managed to grab hold of Saladin's bridle, talking to him all the time. He knows me, you see. He hauled me up a few times—badly frightened, he was—but I stuck until I had him steady, though he was still jumpy and ready to bolt. I tied him to a broken bough so that I could tend to the Squire. He was in a right mess—blood running from his head and over his face, with bits of leaves and twigs stuck to him. His coat was torn and his eyes were shut and he was moaning. I got his foot from the stirrup and laid him down and put my coat over him, then I mounted Saladin. Oh . . . I was sorry about the Squire taking such a fall, but just think, Hester—*me* riding a horse like that one! I just nudged him with my knee, and he sprang away and went like the wind back to the Old Hall.'

Matthew stopped, his eyes shining and his face bright with the memory. He took a sip of the hot water, another bite of oatcake and went on: 'Well, I clattered into the stable-yard, and Hoskett came running, thinking it was the Squire come home. He looked at me as if I was a ghost. Then this girl came running out—she's always round the stables—Miss Olivia, that is, Squire's daughter. She was real bothered and kept grabbing ahold of my elbow and saying: "But where is he? What happened? Where's my father?"'

'Well, the top and tail of it is that we got Jobey to hitch Punch up to the flat cart, and we took the door off the liniment cupboard, then this girl, Miss Olivia, snatched at my arm and rushed me off up to the big house and into her bedroom. I was a bit dumbfounded, I can say; the housekeeper came out on the stairs and threw up her hands and got in the way. Two of the maids came goggling from nowhere. Well, Miss Olivia and me lugged down her mattress and some blankets, and by that time Hoskett and Jobey had got the cart round to the front door, so we threw the things up and jumped on. Do you know, Hester, Miss Olivia wears *boots*, stable boots. Like Jobey's. Funny, isn't it, her all dressed up in one of them pouchy skirts, all fancy, with flowers and bits of lace, then a great, clumping pair o'boots.'

'Well, go on,' I said, impatiently.

'Well, she pushed Jobey off the cart and told him to ride for the doctor so's he'd be there when we got back, and we set off at a great pace. We left the cart at the edge of the wood close by the ride, then Hoskett and I carried in the cupboard door and lifted Squire on to it and carried him back to the cart. Miss Olivia kissed him and cried over him and covered him with blankets. She's real sweet on her father, I'd say. He was talking a bit by then, and it seemed that he thought Saladin had picked up a stone and he was just getting off to look at his hooves when a bird flew out just in front and frightened the horse. He's a nervous one, and he bolted with Squire half on and half off.'

'Is he badly hurt?' I asked.

'And the doctor's horse was there when we got back, so I helped Jobey unhitch Punch, then I came home,' Matthew said, rushing on to the end of the story.

'Is he hurt?' I asked again.

'I dunno. Yes, I suppose he must be. He kept going white when he was talking to Miss Olivia. And she was sobbing and telling Hoskett to mind the bumps in the road . . . I don't know . . . But fancy me riding Saladin!' Matthew laughed proudly and slapped his knee.

We were packed and ready to leave the next day when Mr Hoskett rode up. 'Squire's wanting to see you,' he told Matthew.

'But we're leaving,' I said, quickly. 'We're riding in to Sheffield with the carrier.'

'*He* won't be ready for starting yet. Not until he's seen Betty Gamble.' He laughed, coarsely. 'Look sharp, now,' he said to Matthew, 'and you'll be back the sooner.'

While Matthew was gone I paced restlessly up and down. We *mustn't* miss the carrier. The minutes passed, and I chewed my nails and began to worry. What if the Squire was going to charge Matthew with trespass for being in the wood? Perhaps he thought that *Matthew* had frightened the horse. But no, Matthew had said something about a bird—the Squire had known it was a bird. Perhaps he'd thought Matthew was poaching . . . Or perhaps—I brightened—he was going to reward Matthew. After all, it was possible that Matthew had saved his life. I waited and waited. Surely the carrier would be leaving soon, and time was passing. I could wait no longer. At least I could go to the inn and try and hold him there until Matthew came back.

I was stepping from the rough road on to the causeway near the cottages when I saw Matthew running towards me. At first I thought he was drunk: his face was red, and split into a great grin; then I remembered he hadn't the price of a drink. So I waited. He saw me and waved, then he reached me, and flung his arms around me, swinging me from the ground and almost crushing my bones.

'We've got a house here,' he shouted, 'a nice, tidy little place, and I've got a job in Squire's stables. And he gave me this, too.' He held out a double guinea.

He started to laugh again, triumphantly, against my breast, and Daniel, poor Daniel, squashed between us, began to cry with fright as the last skittle fell with a joyous rattle.

SIX

We moved into Almongate the following morning. My happiness was as full as an overripe plum when summer splits the skin and its sweetness flavours the whole day. There had never been joy like the joy of that November morning.

Hundreds of years ago the land for miles round had belonged to the monks, and our cottage, Almongate, was built where the Almonry Gate had stood. Later, when I learned what an Almoner was, I thought of the beggars who had waited at that place and been helped; their story matched ours; we had come to Stoke Friary with nothing—I without even my strength —and, as in the times long gone, a man's hand had reached out and helped us.

The cottage was built partly of the stone from the old gateway and partly of warm orange brick that seemed to have stored the warmth of years of summer to give it back in the grey days. (Even on the dullest, dampest morning I would look at those bricks, then glance over my shoulder, certain that the sun was slanting across Almongate, only to see that the sky was pewter colour.) And over it all spread a fluted, orange roof.

There was a good sized room downstairs, floored with level stone flags, and a fireplace almost opposite the door. Above were two smaller rooms. Joined to the cottage outside was a little building suitable for a pig or two, and opposite its door was a well set into a circle of cobbles. The front door faced east and opened on to a little garden beyond which a lane ran south from the road down to the river bank. At the back of the cottage a twitchell also linked the same road with the river. And between the road and the river, the lane and the twitchell, lay our land, and there was almost an acre of it.

With the money the Squire had given Matthew we bought the few things we needed: a mattress, two chairs and a table, a cupboard and a few crocks. My mother's ways were mine, and I scoured the latten candlestick and the copper skillet and placed them where they caught the firelight and lit the room.

Then I started to reckon how I could make a real home out of Almongate. I needed more pots and pans, curtains, a few shelves and some matting, and later a cushion or two. For a moment I mourned the earlier bits and pieces I had been forced to sell—if only the double guinea could have bought *those* back. But I didn't waste too much time on moping: there were too many things to do. What I really needed was work for the seven months until the baby came.

Mrs Rowson at the Green Man didn't know of a place for me, but said she'd keep an ear open. She did, however, tell me of a woman, Alice Brackett, who might be willing to take care of Daniel if I got a job where I couldn't have him with me during the day. Like others in the village Mrs Brackett helped her eldest son who worked at home on a stocking-frame, so I went to see her, and she agreed to take Daniel for a few pence each week. So I asked around: did anyone want a maid for dairy or kitchen? No one did.

While I planned I borrowed a spade and started to dig the garden. I brought one of the chairs outside and tied Daniel into it, near me, so that I could talk and sing to him as I worked. I told him of the potatoes and onions that would grow there, of the fowls that would scratch round the pear tree, of the pigs that I hoped to put in the sty. If only I could find a job I could buy seeds and plants and some chicks, and then, by the time the baby was born, the land would be working for us.

With the weather mild and dry, and Matthew out early in the mornings, I could get in a fair stretch of digging, and soon a good sized patch was lying dark and rough and open to the frosts. And then it was January: a day when the wind gulped the air dragging heavy clouds across the sky and knifed the river into grey, jelly-like slices.

I stood with Daniel on the bank watching the barges going down to Hull with their cargoes of coal and pottery and cheese. The grass was flat and winter-grey, and the cold struck up from the frozen ground. The willows crouched as if they, too, felt the chill, and spring seemed far away. I still had no job; perhaps, after all, my garden wouldn't serve me well this year.

I turned back into the north wind and started towards home and I was halfway up the lane when I saw the Squire. I knew it was he because of the great black horse.

I stopped and dropped him my deepest curtsy, nearly unseating Daniel.

The Squire checked his horse and looked down. 'And who are you?' he said, gently.

'Hester Calladine, sir. My husband—'

'Saved my life. Ah, yes. And for that I am indebted—'

'Oh, no, sir. No, indeed.' I rushed on. 'You've allowed us to live in Almongate, and there's the garden and everything.' Then a thought came, and without waiting to ponder the fittingness of it, I said: 'You wouldn't—you don't know of a place for me?' And I could have bitten off my tongue at my boldness.

He was quiet for a moment, displeased, I thought, to be bothered by such a question. 'So you want a place?' he said, at last. 'Don't I pay your husband well enough? There are those who think I'm over-generous in the matter of wages.'

'Oh, *yes*. Indeed you do, sir.' My face flamed. 'I'm not grumbling—I'm very grateful . . . You don't know . . . It's just that—'

'Speak out, Hester Calladine.' He smiled.

I took a breath. 'Well, sir, I haven't enough to do, and there's the land with Almongate. It's good land, but a mite stony . . . I've dug some of it, and it's ready to be raked fine for the spring seeds. I want to use it properly. And then, perhaps, one day, I could have a garden stall in the town and sell what I grow. You see, when you start off with nothing—well, it's not as if we've lived here for years and can harvest some seed or barter a fowl or two. We have to start from the beginning. And I've got the land ready. I'd like to get some chicks and a pig or two. And I haven't any money, and I have nothing to give in exchange for these things. It does seem as though it's wasted—the land.'

He sat watching me, a small smile tipping his mouth, as I stumbled through my tale. My eyes were on his hands, idly smoothing the neck of the great horse, and my words tumbled out foolishly and without a pattern, as if I'd drunk too much.

Then he said: 'Come up to the kitchen of the Old Hall tomorrow morning. Ask to see Mrs Broome.'

I wanted to drop to my knees and kiss the boots that threaded the stirrups, but all I could do was stand there and smile—a smile that must have shown him my back teeth. He looked at me steadily for a moment, and again I felt the hot blood climb into my neck, then he nudged the horse's barrel and said good-day.

I stood in the wintry lane watching him above the proud, glistening rump of Saladin. Slim, but broad-shouldered, not fat and purple-faced like Sir Grenville. He was a gentleman, a *fine* gentleman. Then, smiling, I walked back to Almongate, not feeling the cold, seeing my garden green and growing and filled with food. But against the green rows that my imagination showed me was the blue-coated figure of a man who had looked at me strangely when I smiled, and suddenly I wondered how it would have been if *I* had been in the spinney when his horse bolted, if I had cradled his head and covered him with *my* cloak. And my sense argued back that I couldn't have halted Saladin on his mad rush, nor rode the great beast back to the Old Hall to get help.

And just because a man had a kind face and gentle hands, just because he'd held out hope for a job—was that a reason for admitting such fancies as belonging rightly to spring and a young maiden?

Matthew was angry when I told him. 'You shouldn't have done it, Hester,' he said, with his chin jutting out. 'Bothering gentry like Sir John about a servant's job.'

'I know I shouldn't,' I murmured. 'He just came along while I was thinking, and it was ready on my tongue and the words just dropped off. And . . . I *do* want to get those seeds and some fowls.'

'I'll be able to get enough for our needs,' he said, stiffly.

'Oh, but I want more than that,' I began. 'I've told you—'

'And *I've* told *you*. You can't go setting yourself up as a farmer with these little catchpenny plans of yours. We're new here, and folk won't like it; they'll say you're getting above yourself. And *I* think you're getting greedy, Hester, that's what. Much wants more. Besides, you asking the Squire like that could've cost me my job.'

'But it didn't, did it?' I said, gaily.

'Squire'll think we're not satisfied. Anyway—' Matthew pushed back his chair, '*he'll* think you're greedy.'

Well, I'm not, I wanted to say. And yet, perhaps I am. Greedy for living, for our children that they'll have enough to eat, always. Enough blankets on their beds in winter. So that they can go to the Michaelmas Fair once in a while with more than a penny and not be told to get down on their knees and thank God for their good fortune. I want something else for them, too. And you'd laugh, Matthew, if I told you. I want them to have some schooling. And you'd say: 'Whatever for? What's wrong with things as they are?' Oh, Matthew, have you forgotten so soon what it was like to have nothing? To tramp in the rain and lie in the hedgebottom? That'll never happen to our children if I can help it. And, please God, I *can* help it—with these hands and this brain that He gave me. And with that plot of land that Sir John lets us use.

But aloud I only said: 'You should know me well enough, Matthew, to realize that I wasn't asking for charity. If I get a job at the Old Hall they'll get worth for their money.'

'All the same,' he said, (oh, God wasn't he ever going to stop?) 'you shouldn't have asked Squire a thing like that. It wasn't fitting.'

SEVEN

It was the first time in his nine months that Daniel would be without me, and I felt a sad little pang as I laid him in Alice Brackett's arms the next morning. I felt sick, perhaps because I was leaving him, or because of my pregnancy, or maybe in anticipation of the new job. I stroked his dark, silky hair with my forefinger for a moment, and Alice said, quickly: 'Now, don't you worry; he'll be all right with me. Won't you, my ducky?' She pressed his face into her thin shoulder and smiled at me over his head.

I nodded and smiled back at her, tightly, then I turned to join Matthew who stood at a little distance as if he had no part in the arrangement. I wished I could have shared my muddled feelings with him, wished I could have looked to him for the moment's comfort which I needed, but I knew it was no good. So, as we walked up the slope which led to the Old Hall, I said: 'What's Mrs Broome like? She's the house-keeper, isn't she? The one who came out on the stairs that day when the Squire had his fall and Miss Olivia took you up to her room for the mattress?'

And I was thinking: And that was the last time we were happy together. No, not quite the last time, for there was the day after, when you came running through the village to tell me that we'd got a home. And now, despite the home, despite the job you love with the horses, things are somehow wrong. We're like two ill-tuned fiddles that play together but don't make music.

'Oh, Mrs Broome's well enough,' Matthew said. 'She's a bit strict, and you'll have to watch your tongue with her.'

'And the others?'

'Well, there's Debby . . .'

It was Debby who answered my timid knock and took me into the kitchen, explaining to the stout woman whom I guessed to be the cook, that I'd come to see Mrs Broome.

'Ah. Well, take her in, then.'

Debby led me along a small passage and we stopped outside a door at the end. 'She's in there, Mrs Broome is. Well, you'd better go in.' She gave me a little push. 'That's what you came for, ain't it? Go on—she won't bite.'

I tapped at the door and went in. Mrs Broome was sitting at a small round table, an open Bible before her. She was a fat woman who overflowed her chair; she had a rosy face and should, to my way of thinking, have been jolly-looking, but instead she was sad, as if she'd laid on flesh like thick, drab clothing. Her jaw sagged like a hound's dewlaps, and her eyes were set in dark, drooping pouches.

'Well,' she asked in a sighing, breathy voice, 'what can you do?'

'I'll do anything, Ma'am,' I said, willingly.

She was silent, and I wondered if I'd sounded too jaunty. I began again: 'There were three of us in my last place. Between us we did the housework, laundry, ironing and mending and some dairy work as well.'

'There'll be no dairy work here,' she said. 'This is not a farm.'

'No, Ma'am.'

Slowly she heaved herself out of her chair. From a chest she took out a white mop-cap threaded with grey ribbon, a white apron and a bigger one of coarse, brown stuff. She opened a cupboard and unhooked two grey print dresses and shook them out, looking me over and shaking her head. 'Much too small,' she said.

'These won't do at all. Too short to be decent.' She looked accusingly at me as if I were to blame for my height. 'You'll have to have two of the new ones. And as you will not be living in the Hall I shall expect you to keep them clean and in good state.'

'Yes, Ma'am,' I said, feeling that I had committed yet another crime by not living in.

'Very well. That is all.'

'But what shall I— What are my duties?'

'You will help Mrs Hayes for the time being. I must say, engaging maids without so much as a word to me . . .' Then she smiled suddenly.

I closed the door quietly—the hushed mood of the room had affected me, too, then I went back down the passage to the kitchen. I stood inside the doorway uncertainly. Then I swallowed, lifted my head and went forward. 'I'm Hester Calladine,' I said. 'I've got to help Mrs Hayes.'

'That's right,' said the stout woman. 'I'm Mrs Hayes, the cook. But draw up a stool, do. We always have a mug of ale about this time. This here is Annie Fletcher, the saucy one that let you in is Debby, and them two at the end of the table are Betty and Poll.'

I nodded and smiled at them, then laid my pile of clothes on the enormous black dresser which took up most of one wall. I pulled up a stool, and Mrs Hayes drew me a mug of ale from the keg in the corner.

The girl called Annie said: 'I see you got the new high-waisted gowns. You'd think that them as has been here longest would have got 'em. But no. Everything's done topsy-turvey here, and I allus knew Sir John had his favourites.'

'Now, Annie, none of that talk,' Mrs Hayes said. 'It's no way to make a start.' Then, turning to me, she said: 'Don't you pay no note to our Annie—she's got a rare nip of frost to her tongue these cold mornings. And stop your scowling, Annie.'

'Yes, stop screwing your face up. If Jack Hallam could see you now . . .' That was Debby. 'He took her to the fair, he did,' she explained to me. 'Years ago, it was, and they're still not wed. Course, he's got better things to do has our Jack.' She laughed. Annie's face was a dull red, and she shot Debby a poisonous glare.

'Well, never mind all that,' Mrs Hayes said, comfortably. 'You're too cheeky by half, Deb. And good wine's all the better for keeping, eh, Annie?' She twinkled at me and gave a slight shrug as if to say: I'm hard pushed to keep the peace here, sometimes.

'Let's have a look at these dresses,' said the one called Betty, going over to the dresser and holding up one of the stiff, unfaded gowns. 'Yes, quite the style, ain't they, Poll? Reckon I'll have to scorch my old 'un, then maybe Broomstick'll give me one like this.'

'And I'll dob a bit of tar on mine and get a new one, too,' Poll laughed.

'You'll do no such thing,' Mrs Hayes exclaimed, wiping her mouth with the back of her hand. 'There's naught wrong with the one's you've got. Years of wear left in 'em.'

'*That's* what's wrong with them,' Betty said.

'But you won't be needing them much longer unless you get along to your work,' went on Mrs Hayes. 'Mrs Broome'll be after you if you don't get along. You know what happened last week.'

'Well, she shouldn't go trailing her fingers into dark corners,' Debby said. 'Besides, she won't pay us much heed today. She'll be too busy with God: she went to a preaching last night.' All the same, she pushed back her stool and started collecting the dirty mugs.

Mrs Hayes got up from the table. 'Now,' she said to me, 'you'd better get changed, then you can start on the vegetables. And after that you'd better tidy up the store cupboard for I can't lay a hand to anything.'

I was pleased with the new high-waisted gowns for surely they would hide my shape better than the older ones which the girls were wearing. I didn't want Mrs Broome to see my state too soon; it might give her an excuse to get rid of me.

When I'd finished tidying the cupboard and had brushed out the spillings of salt and flour Mrs Hayes came to look.

'Now, *that's* something like,' she said. 'A right airy-fairy is Deb. If she'd less wits in her tongue and more in her hands that cupboard would never have got into such a state. You can clean the knives now, duck. It'll be a rare treat for 'em.'

Her approval gladdened me. With Daniel safely lodged with Alice Brackett, Matthew happy in the stables, myself earning a wage and, to cap it all, working for such a kindly woman as Mrs Hayes, my early glumness lifted.

There were four of the family living at the Old Hall: Sir John and Lady Lindsey, Miss Olivia and Master Roland. The older son, Mr Dominic, was away in Italy, Mrs Hayes said. The tightness of her lips as she spoke of him told me that, in her opinion, that country was welcome to him.

I met Miss Olivia on my second day. It was her duty to take her mother's chocolate up every morning and to wait to bring the cup back. No one but she was permitted to handle that cup; it was thin and fragile with a pattern of birds and insects painted round the side, and the knob on the cover was fashioned like a bullfinch. Miss Olivia must rinse and dry it, afterwards putting it away in a cupboard where it had a tiny shelf to itself.

She was always cheerful when she came into the kitchen to take down the cup, asking after Mrs Hayes's bad legs, teasing Deb, or playing with the cat. When she returned with the empty cup, however, her mood was quite different. Sometimes there were tear-trails on her face, sometimes she was sullen, and once she stood, weighing the cup in her hand as if she would dash it to the floor.

One day after Olivia had banged out to the stables to find her father, I said to Mrs Hayes: 'What happens to change her so? When she first comes in she's full of smiles and chat and picking bits off the crust. Then, when she comes back, she's a real thundercloud.'

'Ah, well, it's her Ladyship, you see.'

'Why? I don't see . . . You mean she gets angry with Miss Olivia perhaps? Every morning?'

'Angry. Well, not so much that . . . If you ask me, it's done as a torment.'

I was trying hard to understand. Sometimes, listening to Mrs Hayes was like trying to catch smoke. 'Why should she torment Miss Olivia? What's she done?'

'Oh, it's not what she's *done*; it's more what she's *not* done . . . She's twenty-two, duck, and not showing any inclination to get wed. Very strong on her father, is Miss Olivia. She's his pet . . . And knowing the others you can't wonder. Mister Dominic'll never amount to much—not that he's any worse than a lot of the gentry, though there *is* something downright nasty about him that I can't put my finger on . . . And as for Master Roland . . .' She shook her head, sadly.

But I wanted to hear more about Miss Olivia who wore stableboys' boots beneath her fine dresses—although somehow they never looked so fine on her: there was usually a torn frill, a button wrongly fastened or gaping, a sash creased and carelessly knotted. 'Well,' I said, 'I still don't see what kind of torment it is for a girl to take up her mother's chocolate.'

'Well, no, you wouldn't. You don't know Lady Lindsey. She's got a way with her of making you feel you're wrong even when you know you're right. Thank the Lord she doesn't concern herself much with *us*— she leaves that to Mrs Broome. But since her last maid left she can't get another one, and that means Miss Olivia has to dress her hair sometimes and do other little jobs for her so they're thrown together more than they were. Anyway, *I* think her Ladyship gets Miss Olivia up there, waiting for her to finish drinking the chocolate, spinning it out no doubt to last as long as it can, and all the while she's going on at the poor

girl about her hair, the state of her clothes, her be-
haviour, the way she's always hanging about the
stables. You know the kind of thing,' she said, wagging
a spoon, 'like when you keep a bird in a cage just so
you can take a poke at it when you fancy and watch
it flutter.'

'But that's cruel,' I said, disbelieving.

'Aye. That's just what it is. Once Miss Olivia had
her own maid, a nice little thing—Lucy her name was.
And when the mistress saw that Miss Olivia had grown
fond of Lucy she sent her packing. Said she'd stolen
some spoons. But I notice she didn't bring a charge
against her, and I'll lay them spoons are somewhere in
her Ladyship's room. Awful what jealousy will do.'

'Jealousy?' I said, chasing after her words.

'Now isn't that what I've been talking about? Her
Ladyship's jealous because the Squire spends more
time with Miss Olivia than he does with her. Go tell
Tom to bring in more potatoes, there's a duck—these
are all green.'

Master Roland's birthday fell on my second Tuesday
at the Old Hall. There was to be a party in the nursery,
and several of the children from the big houses in the
neighbourhood were to come for a special supper in
honour of the day. The pasties and cakes had been
made the day before, the jellies were made early on
the Tuesday morning and had been put to set in the
coldroom. All that remained was for the biggest, plum-
miest cake to be 'tricked up' as Mrs Hayes put it.

She had her usual afternoon nap in her chair by the
fire while I mopped the floor, and when she awoke and
saw that all was clean and tidy she told me to get out
the almond paste which had been made ready, and
from a drawer in the dresser she took out a little
pottery mould shaped like a chicken.

'Miss Goodbody bought this in London,' she said.
'Master Roland loves chickens. I well remember when
one got into the garden. There he was chasing it,

clucking and mewing and flapping his arms—squawking with laughter so you were hard put to know which was boy and which was fowl. Miss Goodbody has her hands full with him, I can tell you.'

I watched Mrs Hayes roll out the almond paste and stamp out several chicken shapes. 'Now, just trail a bit of that preserve over the cake, Hester,' she said. 'That'll make 'em stick.'

'Don't you think—'

'What, ducky?'

'They'd look better with eyes. We could use bits of raisins,' I suggested, timidly.

'Now, why ever didn't I think of that. You do the eyes, then.'

'And with what's left of the paste we could make a few little eggs and heap them in the middle.'

'You do it,' she said, approvingly.

'Who's Miss Goodbody?' I asked as I rolled the egg shapes between my palms.

'She's Master Roland's nurse. Ain't you seen her? No, she hasn't been down lately. Well, she's a governess, really, but of course he don't do no lessons. She takes him for walks—I'm surprised you haven't seen 'em, but perhaps they haven't been down your way. They go gathering leaves and berries and such to stick in books. There's a great stack of them berry books upstairs. She's very good with him is Miss Goodbody; she gets him making little things from beads and paper and such. It keeps him quiet.'

'What's she like?'

'Oh—pale, big-eyed, thin enough to snap in two when the wind blows. Got no style about her at all.'

'It's a small family, just three children.'

'There should've been eight. Five died before their fourth birthday.'

I put the last egg carefully on the cake.

'Well, I call that right pretty,' Mrs Hayes said. 'He *will* be pleased, bless him.'

As I cleared the table I pictured the scene up in the

nursery. The curtains would be drawn against the dusk, and the fire would blaze and waver along the steel fender. The table, spread with a white cloth, would show up clearly the fruit colours of the jellies— the colours children like: red, green, yellow and orange. And clustered round would be the little girls in their silks and muslins, pink-cheeked from warmth and excitement, ribbons slipping from silky curls; and the boys, in frilled shirts and buckled shoes and cleaner than they liked to be. And, at the centre, Master Roland, the handsomest child of all, spreading chubby fingers in delight that his beloved chickens had come to his birthday supper.

I wondered if he looked like his father and Miss Olivia. I wondered if Miss Olivia would be there in the nursery, and if her father and mother would be there, too, linked and close because it was a family celebration.

I was about to leave for home when a tall youth banged into the kitchen dragging by the wrist a pale, thin woman.

'Master Roland would like to thank you for the birthday cake,' she gasped to Mrs Hayes. 'Come along, Roland,' she smiled encouragingly at the boy's sweet, empty face. 'Say "thank you" to Mrs Hayes for the chickens.'

He began to speak, but it was as if his jaw had slipped, and the noises he made were not words. His slow, piercing black eyes swivelled round the room as if searching for something until they rested on the brown crock on the dresser. He began to gibber and point.

'Bless him,' said Mrs Hayes, moving forward, 'he wants a gingerbread dolly. There you are, my lamb.'

The boy took the sweetmeat and crammed it into his mouth, laughing, spraying dark crumbs over Miss Goodbody's thin bosom. Then he spun round and, as suddenly as they came, they were gone.

I was still where I stood when they came in, one

hand frozen on its way to my hood. I looked at Mrs
Hayes. 'You should have told me,' I said softly, sadly.
'I had been picturing a children's party . . . the chick-
ens and everything—'

'It was a children's party,' she said. 'His friends are
children. Fifteen years today he is, but it's only his
body that's grown. The rest of him is a child. Proper
tragic. Two boys and neither of 'em what they should
be, one way and another. So now you know why
Squire sets such store by Miss Olivia.'

EIGHT

The days I spent working in the kitchen were like the pattern of spilled beads: no matter how often they fall their order is always different. And so it was with me, for although much of the work must be done again and again, no two days were quite alike.

Mrs Hayes wasn't at all like my mother, yet there was something maternal about her. She was easy and comfortable, unsparing with her praise when I worked well—so, of course, I tried to please. In many houses the cooks ruled the kitchen with spite, and a kitchen maid's job could be misery. I was fortunate, and I knew it. Now, when I look back on those days I see there was a happy simplicity about them, a flavour that never quite came again.

Master Roland recognized me now when he rushed in. I knew what he came for, and when I reached for the big crock he'd gibber and squeak like a puppy who knows where his bone is kept. Childlike and beautiful, with those great, lustrous eyes, he'd watch me lift the lid. He'd smile, and my heart would shrink with pity. I gave him the sweetmeat and brushed his smooth cheek with my finger tips. Perhaps he was unused to affection, for he didn't cram the gingerbread into his mouth as he did when Mrs Hayes gave it to him, but stood, watching my face. Then he'd offer his cheek, and I'd kiss him, and he'd put up his hand, wonderingly, to touch the place. It must have been a bitter thing for Lady Lindsey to have a son so comely to look at, yet so senseless to know, and I often won-

dered if her treatment of Miss Olivia had its root in
Master Roland's lack. But this was just one of my idle
thoughts as I scoured pans and scrubbed vegetables
for I had seen her Ladyship but twice and then only
at a distance.

One Saturday afternoon when Mrs Hayes was sleeping, quietly 'pluffing' in her chair, Mrs Broome sent
for me and told me in her mournful way that on the
following Monday my place in the kitchen was to be
taken by a young girl from the poorhouse, and in
future I must work with Annie.

Although I was pleased at this chance to see more
of the hall and more of the family—I might even get a
glimpse of Sir John—I sensed that Annie wouldn't
welcome my company. She never lost an opportunity
to carp at me, mocking the way I spoke, pretending
she couldn't understand my 'outlandish tongue.' In
the kitchen I'd soon got her measure and was able to
keep out of her way much of the time, but now this
would not be possible. I was surprised, therefore,
when on the Monday, as we polished the stairs, Annie
asked, quite civilly, if I liked living at Almongate.

'Oh, *yes*,' I said, squatting back on my heels for a
moment. 'It's a trim, cosy little place. I like Stoke
Friary altogether.'

'I thought you must. It was a good way of getting
somewhere to live, wasn't it, after being chucked out
of your other place.'

I stared at her, but her head was bent as her hand
went back and forth across the polished treads, and I
couldn't see her face.

'Getting somewhere to live? I don't understand—'

'Well,' she said, and now she looked at me, and her
eyes were sharp with spite, 'I'll tell you, then. There's
folk who say your husband threw a stone, and *that's*
what frightened Squire's horse that day in the spinney.'

I almost laughed, but something in her face stopped
me. 'Why would Matthew want to do a thing like
that?'

'Why, you ninny, it's clear, ain't it? So's he could go rushing out, all brave like, and stop the horse and save the Squire. Everyone knows that your husband *knew* that horse and could likely deal with it.'

I stared, then began to laugh. 'Well, whoever's saying that has got more fancy than fact. Matthew would never—'

'Well, you couldn't blame him, could you?' she went on as if I hadn't spoken. 'I mean, you coming here with no money nor nothing. It was a good chance. He must be a sharp one, your husband.'

Matthew sharp? I opened my mouth to answer but the hatred in her face shocked me. She thought, perhaps, that she'd frightened me, and as we moved down to the next stair a sneaky little smile lifted her mouth. 'And I'll tell you sommat else. Even if you hadn't got Almongate out of it all, who's to say that the two silver buttons missing from Squire's coat weren't torn off and kept by that husband of yours? Stolen.'

'Well, don't kneel there looking like an idiot,' she went on. 'Your husband could've ripped them off and kept them, the Squire being in such poor case as not to know what was happening. And afterwards he would think the buttons came off while he was being dragged along.'

'You're crazed,' I said. 'If Matthew'd done that and been caught it might have meant transportation. He wouldn't risk that for two little silver buttons.'

'Ho. "Two little silver buttons" she says. You talk as if they were pebbles. Folk've risked it for less as you don't need me to tell you. Anyway,' she picked up her rag and moved down a stair, 'it's what they're saying.'

'Who? Who are saying it?'

But she didn't answer, just tossed her head and tried to look wise. Suddenly I felt sure that she'd made the whole thing up. But why? 'Annie,' I began, 'what—'

'Oh, come *on*, for pity's sake, or we'll never get done. *I* haven't got time to talk, and neither have you.'

I had a great urge to shake her until the truth rattled out, but the early sickness stayed with me until almost noon and, nauseated by the smell of the polish and my own baffled fury, I felt limp for a moment. All I wanted to do was to get the stairs finished and run to the kitchen door and gulp down great breaths of the cold morning air.

Later that day when I caught Mrs Hayes alone I asked her why Annie disliked me so much.

'Ah, well, you got Almongate, didn't you?' she said, as if that explained everything.

'But I don't see why she should hold that against me.'

'Then I'll tell you, duck. Annie's all right in her way, but she's a mite sour. She's been set on Jack Hallam for years. Like Polly told you, he once took her to the Michaelmas Fair, so Annie thought they were set to wed. Perhaps they would have if they could have found a place to live. When Almongate fell empty Annie's mother was going to speak to Squire about it. That would have brought Jack Hallam to the point maybe. But Annie's mother wasn't quick enough. You came along, Squire had that fall in the spinney—well, you know the rest. So Jack won't wed until they find a place here to live, and if you ask me I don't reckon he's in such a hurry as our Annie. It's all she thinks of, but him—well, he's always on the edge of trouble is Jack. I reckon Annie thinks marriage would settle him a bit— But . . . there you are, and that's the way of it. So now you know why she hasn't taken to you.'

'But I . . .' I shrugged.

'Now, don't you go letting it worrit you, Hester. Annie's just like her mother: always got to have her grumble and grudge, and if it wasn't against you it'd be some poor soul else.'

'Is Jack Hallam wild, then?' I asked.

'Not wild after women or drink. Naught like that. He's—well, he's a nice lad, really, but a bit of a firebrand. Got a lot of new ideas, like talking against the gentry, and that. Can't keep a job long, though they say he's a good worker, but he hasn't the sense to keep his mouth shut. And Annie's so set on him, and she's not getting any younger. Still, there's nothing any of us can do about that, is there?'

One of my new jobs was to keep Miss Olivia's room tidy. I did this during the hour she spent with her mother or while she took breakfast with her father in the small parlour. I'd grown to like her although she wasn't what I'd have expected of a lady.

She looked rather like a squirrel with her reddish-brown hair drawn back, caught at the top of her head with a crumpled ribbon, to fall in a thick, waving tail. When she smiled (and she had a very sweet smile that made her look like her father), one side of her mouth tilted and pointed to a dimple, and her cheeks plumped up into little pink pouches. Yes, just like a squirrel: shy, a little wild and perhaps a little fierce at times; but whereas squirrels are neat, smooth-shaped little creatures, Miss Olivia was untidy. And that was perhaps why Annie had given me the task of cleaning her room.

It was at the back of the house and hadn't been done over like most of the other rooms when the alterations had been made some years ago. It was quite small and gloomy, with a sloping floor of wide planks and a ceiling so low my head nearly touched the beams. The single window was small, with tiny panes of thick greenish glass.

It took more time to clean than any of the other rooms, and Miss Olivia was careless: one day I even found a ring caught between two floor planks under the bed. I hooked it out and laid it on the small table by her bed, then I noticed the book lying there. I turned the pages slowly, wondering how a person could get a tale from the tiny, jumbled marks. I put it down when I heard the door open and turned sharply, misjudging the distance between the table and my hand. The book clattered to the floor, and I stood, clutching my duster guiltily.

Miss Olivia looked cross. She'll scold like a squirrel, I thought, but she just flopped on to the bed, chewing her lip. I bent to replace the book, then she saw me.

'Have you been reading?' she asked, without interest.

'Why no, miss. I can't.'

'Then count yourself lucky,' she said.

'How can that be?' I answered, forgetting my place. 'When there is something to know and books can tell you—can you be better off not knowing?'

'A judicious reply,' she said, looking at me sharply. 'But consider this: by knowing a thing one is shown how life could be, might be, but so rarely is.'

I didn't understand her remark, but I glimpsed the despair behind it. Still, I thought, who would choose not to read, given a choice? '*I* should like to be able to read,' I said softly and moved towards the door.

A few days later I was leaving her room, having finished my work there, when she came along the passage. She'd been crying; her eyes were red, and she looked wretched. As I passed her she caught my wrist and drew me back into the room.

'Are you good with a needle?' she said, in a low voice.

'I sew well enough, I believe, miss.'

'Could you stitch this?' She held up her wrist and I saw the frayed cuff.

'Yes, I think so.'

'Very well.' She composed her face, smoothed her hair and turned to look out of the window. 'I've got lots of gowns like this. Lots. Nearly all, in fact. My mother could tell you. Buttons missing, frills torn. She has a woman who comes to repair her clothing . . . You take care of my clothes and I'll teach you to read.' Her voice had changed to one of stubborn purpose.

'Oh, I don't think I could,' I said. 'What would Mrs Broome say? I have to help Annie.'

'I'll speak to Mrs Broome.' I could see how she'd be if she were mistress in her own house: dignified, stern, but reasonable. 'I'm not permitted a maid of my own, yet it distresses my mother to see me "in tatters". One small tear and she calls it "tatters". And I must "remedy the matter". And so I shall. Well? You *want* to read, don't you?'

'Oh, *yes*.' Even if it meant being a part of her quarrel with her mother, for I sensed this was the core of the matter.

'Very well. I shall teach you. Come to my room this afternoon and every afternoon from three o'clock until four. I shall see that you're spared for an hour— Broomey likes me. But not a word about the reading to anyone. It must be a secret, otherwise you'll suddenly be surprised to hear you've been at the silver, and you'll find yourself without a job. You must just tell them that you've been put to sewing upstairs.'

'Yes, Miss Olivia.'

'Very well, Hester. Come up at three o'clock and we'll make a start.'

I was excited when I went up to her room that same afternoon. To read! Sir Grenville in Saxtoft hadn't allowed anyone on the Waste to learn to read, although a few had managed it somehow. The parson had been willing to teach, but Sir Grenville believed—like many of the gentry—that reading was only for those with money and therefore time; the poor should be busy, therefore they had no time. My own thoughts reasoned also that if the gentry were the only ones who could read it kept them that bit wiser than the others, like someone who guards his skill lest sharing should cheapen its value. And so I was excited. But yet I was timid because I might prove too stupid to master it. That would be worse than never having tried . . . I pulled myself up sharply and tapped on the door.

82   SO WILD A LOVE

Miss Olivia had pinned scraps of paper to some of
the things in her room, and on each scrap she'd written a mark. She explained that the marks on the three
pieces which were pinned to the bed spelled the word
'bed'. There was also 'wall' and 'hat'.

'Now,' she said, 'I want you to look at those pieces
of paper and remember the shape of the marks on
them. Each mark is a letter and has a sound. Several
sounds put together make a word. As you sew keep
looking until you think you can remember each
mark.'

I sat on the edge of the bed stitching round a
frayed buttonhole, glancing up as I drew the thread
and staring at the marks until they had written themselves across my eyes.

After a while she unpinned the pieces of paper and
gave them to me. 'Now, Hester, I want you to put the
pieces that spell "bed" back on the bed. See if you can
do it.'

I sorted through the scraps and did as she said, although I got the 'b' and the 'd' mixed.

'Now the others.' It seemed a difficult game. 'That's
good,' she said in the tone I sometimes used with
Daniel. 'Now you must say the sound of each mark,
but we will not call them marks, but letters or charac-
ters. Am I going too quickly for you? See—I'll show
you—buh eh duh, b-e-d, bed. You see?'

I had some trouble with the word 'wall' for the 'a'
had a different sound from the 'a' in hat, but after a
time I began to master it, and then it was four o'clock
and the room was growing dark.

'You've done very well, Hester. You have a natural
talent. You can go now.'

'But, Miss Olivia,' I said, 'I shall never do it. All
those hundreds of words in the book there—I'll never
find time to learn them all.' It seemed that the whole
of my life wouldn't give time enough, and I only had
until June when the baby would be born.

Her dimple came, then the laugh. 'I'm sorry, Hester, I'm a clumsy teacher—I should have explained. I expect I've begun at the wrong end, as usual, only this way seemed more interesting . . . Look, there are only twenty-six letters to learn, and for a different word we use the same letters, perhaps, but arrange them differently. Do you understand? No? Well, if I take the duh from bed and change it with the tuh from hat then we have two more words, bet and had. Now do you see? Look at this book—here,' she pointed to a word, 'and here.' She pointed to another word. 'Both words are different, but they both use two of the same letters. You'll understand after a week or two.'

I was more confused than ever now.

During the evenings after Matthew had gone to the Green Man I sat nursing Daniel and learning my letters, for Miss Olivia had given me a paper with them all written large and clear. She gave me a quill, too, and showed me how to use it, and after six weeks I copied my name. I had never realized what a long name it was, but it was some time before I lost my fear of the quill. It was my enemy, it would brook no mistake: once a letter was made it was there, real and black, shouting at me from the paper. But after I had learned to manage it more easily, it was pure pleasure to watch the words creep from under the point and make their message for all to read. When I wrote my first sentence 'My hat is red' Miss Olivia clapped her hands and said: 'I'm an excellent tutor—or you are a gifted pupil. The latter, I suspect.'

So the days were threaded with satisfaction as my learning advanced, word by tiny word.

One morning, when Annie was crying with the face-ache, I was sent upstairs to light the fire in the room adjoining Lady Lindsey's bedroom, which could be reached from a door on the gallery.

I was working quietly as I'd been bade when a petulant voice called: 'Do make haste, Olivia. What are

you doing out there, for heaven's sake? You know
that Mrs Cleland is coming . . . Must I wait all morning for you? One would think that at least—'

I got up from my knees and tapped on the door of
her room.

'Come in, come in, for God's sake.'

I opened the door. 'It's not Miss Olivia, my lady. I'm
doing the fire. Do you wish me to bring her?'

'Yes, yes. First pull the curtains back.'

I crossed the thick gloom of the room which
smelled of scent and powder and dog and that stuffy,
dry sourness of a bed which has been too long slept
in. As I drew back the silk curtains the grey morning
light sifted in, showing the toilet table laid with glass
and porcelain and silver. The ceiling was painted in
white and gold and green, and the carpet had a pattern of lilies. The hangings of the bed matched the
curtains—green, embroidered with gold and black
peonies and edged with fat, gold tassels. It was very
grand.

The light showed, too, mercilessly, the dry-looking
hair tumbling from its stiffened, fashionable shape under the muslin bag, the grubby bedgown slipping from
her fat shoulders. It showed the stained bedcover,
probably the work of the little dog which snored and
bubbled on a tiny, elegant stool. It showed a face
once beautiful, but now scarred with downward-run-
ning lines of ill-humour in which paint still held to the
yellowish skin. Lady Lindsey was very stout, not very
clean and extremely ill-tempered.

'I'll bring Miss Olivia,' I murmured and slipped out.
As I hurried along the gallery I wondered—and was
ashamed and surprised at myself for wondering—if Sir
John paid many visits to that room, if he breathed the
stale air and lifted the stained coverlet and . . .

Then, with a sudden lift of relief, I decided he
didn't. He wouldn't. He, too, would find it, and her,
unpleasing, unwholesome.

NINE

The year reached for spring. Violet dawns paled to pearly green and for a while watched themselves in the splintered white mirrors of ice-pools. Then gradually the iron-ribbed earth softened, and I had to kilt my skirt about my knees against the muddy lane as I walked with Matthew up to the Old Hall.

Then spring came; timidly at first, fingering her way up through the quickening soil. Tightly-rolled catkins swung from the birches, new yellow pricked the buff willows. The season took on sureness with the lengthening days, and we no longer needed the lantern to show the path, for as soon as we turned off the road the stone urn that marked the front east corner of the Old Hall's roof stood out clearly in the early light, then a few minutes later, the clipped bird-shapes of the yews were revealed. Beyond the park where the ground rose, the trees and hedges bloomed with the soft beginnings of green.

Matthew and I didn't talk much as we made our way up the lane. It seemed that, as soon as we closed the door of Almongate behind us, Matthew was reminded afresh that I had taken this job, and he was silent until he placed Daniel into Alice Brackett's arms; then, as we left the main street to climb the gentle slope he'd grumble: 'Don't know why you want to turn out like this of a morning. We've got a home, and we can grow all *we* need. My mother did what my father told her to do, but you . . . And she was none the worse for it. There's naught wrong with the old ways . . .'

I'd smother a sigh for I had tried so many times to make him understand. But I'd try again and tell him that I did it for the good of all of us.

'Why?' He'd jut his chin. 'Why must you have a garden-stall in town? What will be the end of it all?'

'It's something I *must* do, Matthew. Don't you see? It's a chance for Daniel and this other baby to have a little more than we had. Is that so strange?'

'If you had your way, and if all folk thought like you, then every man Jack would be a gentleman. Then where would we all be? You've got to know your place, Hester, and stop in it.'

'Every man Jack *couldn't* be a gentleman,' I protested. 'That takes generations—good food, education, breeding—and then something extra.' My thoughts would turn, naturally, but disturbingly, to Sir John and that cold January afternoon.

'But we only need so much each day, Hester, and I can find that. Be thankful for it, for pity's sake, and stop forever seeking something more.'

At those times it seemed that he knew me better than I'd supposed, for, when I looked back, in everything I did I had sought 'something more'. I saw Almongate as something to *begin* with, to go on from, while Matthew was still blessing the luck that had brought us here and given him his job. I wanted to remind him of the two servants in the Bible who had used their master's talents wisely; from where my thoughts went back to that man—Morland—at the inn in Flewster. He'd used his talents well, for his kind eyes and soft voice had stripped us of our money, although unwittingly he'd done us a good turn: had it not been for him we should now be in Sheffield. Recalling him I'd remember how, before he robbed us, he'd prayed with us that we might be brought to the Promised Land. They say women in my state have strange fancies, and perhaps this was the reason I regarded our scant acre bound by the lane and the twitchell, the high road and the river, as the Promised Land, as something holy.

Apart from the flyaway fancies of thought and appetite that come with the time of breeding, there is something else: the looking inwards. I did a lot of this. My reading was improving, my little hoard of money mounting. I loved my work at the Old Hall. I loved Mrs Hayes and Miss Olivia. I had made a friend of Master Roland, and although it was a strange kind of friendship where no words passed, he would make a noise that could be taken as 'Hester' and stand quietly holding the gingerbread, until I kissed him. So they were good days with life quickening within me and around. I seemed linked to the earth with the promise of fullness, and beyond this most other things were of small matter.

But, in a way, it was an unreal state. Because I was begetting life I tended to see myself as the centre of living. Yet affairs everywhere were changing, although I knew this only from the scraps of gossip which I heard from the servants and Miss Olivia, or from Matthew when he came home from the Green Man or the town. To those who cannot read, the inn and market-place are messengers, so talk was free and most things were thoroughly chewed apart in their telling.

I had never been into the town, but Matthew had told me a little about it: of the castle that topped a great rock, only, he said, it wasn't really a castle, but a grand mansion. There were other beautiful, though smaller houses, many alehouses, an Assembly Room and an Exchange overlooking a vast market-place. It was in this market-place during the Michaelmas Fair twenty years ago that trouble had broken out over the price of cheese, and cheeses were snatched from stalls and flung about, one even bowling over the Mayor. People still talked of this, reckoning time from that date, saying: 'He was born during the Cheese Fair.' Once, when Polly dropped and broke two kitchen plates, one after the other, Mrs Hayes had rounded on her, shouting: 'No call to toss 'em like cheeses at a fair.'

There had been other troubles in the market-place since then; folk always gather there at such times. Last year about the price of butter, and earlier when the wages for stocking work dropped. At both times the Militia had been called in to keep order.

There was still some bitterness over the loss of the American Colonies, and nearer, in France, there was unrest. But I heard these things as if they had been told to me in that moment before waking when time and the mind are mixed. I was more interested in what was happening in the fastness of my own world, and it was my world I thought about after I left Matthew at the path which turned off to the stables.

The trees at the top of the hill caught the wind and scratched at the April skies. I walked briskly for it was cold, and I was eager for the afternoon when I would show Miss Olivia my progress. She'd written a book for me, and I had read it. It was the first whole book I'd ever read, and although she'd used only the simplest words and it was only a few pages long I hugged it to me beneath my old cloak, thinking with satisfaction of the pleasure she'd show when I read it to her.

I was humming softly as I carried a pile of linen upstairs, not knowing that Olivia was standing in an alcove on the gallery arranging some daffodils in a big blue bowl.

'You sound happy,' she said.

'Oh, good morning, miss.' I stopped. 'They're lovely. Stiff and clean and . . . well . . . untouched.'

'Immaculate,' she said, crisply, tweaking a stem into place. 'I'm going away to London, Hester. But come up this afternoon, as usual.' She sounded annoyed, so when I went to her I tapped at the door a little nervously. 'Come in.' She was throwing clothes into two boxes which stood open on the floor of her room. In one a heap of shoes had been hurled, pell-mell; the other held a pile of badly-folded gowns.

'Help me pack, Hester,' she said, cramming a lacy shawl down the side of a box. 'Damn it to hell and beyond, I'll never get this lot in. Why in heaven's name I must be touted around London again I'll never know. I'd hoped last year would be the end of it. Don't stand there, Hester, hand me that green dress . . . Or don't you think I should take it? Oh, damnation.' She pushed her hands through her untidy hair and stood helplessly.

'Let me do it,' I said. 'You lay out the clothes you want to take; I'll pack them.' I began to take out the crumpled dresses, folding them more neatly.

'This, and this, I think . . .' She was throwing hats on to the bed. 'I *don't* want to go to London. I *don't* want to pack. So why the devil can't I be left alone.'

I almost laughed. There was something comic about her anger, but when she turned and the light fell on her face, I was glad I hadn't. She'd been crying. 'They do say London is a fine city,' I began, carefully not looking at her.

'I know what it's like. I get hauled off there every year.'

I was silent, then, after a moment, I said: 'I'm sorry you're going.'

'So am I. You don't know how sorry.'

'This is very sudden-like, isn't it?' I asked, afraid of seeming too curious.

'It's one of Mother's pleasant surprises,' she said, bitterly. 'I'm to have a try at finding a husband. Like a beast entered for the Fatstock Show I might—if I'm lucky—bring home a prize.'

'Oh, miss,' I said, 'it's surely not that way.'

'It is. It's exactly that way.'

There was much that was childlike about her, for she hadn't yet learned the tricks of speech and face of so many ladies, nor had she had to meet life with sense and fortitude as other less fortunate women had.

And now the child part of her was uppermost, small, sad and tear-stained.

I said, gently, 'Perhaps London will be better than you remember. Sometimes places are. Isn't it very gay, with lots to see and everyone dressed so splendid? And aren't there theatres and balls and concerts and pleasure-gardens?'

'Oh, yes.' She mimicked my voice. 'There are gin- and hanging-parties. Duels and Bedlam. Beggars and starving children. All manner of entertainments.' Then a shadow of her dimple came. 'I *am* making a tangle of it, but—oh, I just wish life could go on as it is now. Why must it be changed? I'm happy here—most of the time.'

'Sometimes change is for the better.'

'Oh, Hester, don't keep trying to soothe me with platitudes.'

'But you might meet a handsome, rich gentleman,' I suggested, 'then you'd be pleased you went.'

'Perhaps.'

Dislike for Lady Lindsey rose like bile. All the little ways in which she tormented Miss Olivia came back to me: her tinkling little laugh that damned Miss Olivia's opinions, the stupid cruel business of the daily chocolate. Her words, carried from the dining-room by one of the maids: 'If you cannot get to the table promptly, Olivia, you might at least get the stink of stable-litter off you first.' The voice that snapped like a stretched cord shouting along the gallery: 'It's your father's doing. You're not a girl at all! You should have been off my hands years ago—get back to the animals where you belong.'

Yet it couldn't always have been this way, for young daughters, if they were pretty and accomplished and pleasant, were treasures; they could be married off well, enlarging an estate, perhaps bringing money where it was wanted. But Miss Olivia—it was getting late for her.

I rolled some gloves and tucked them into a corner of the trunk.

'Come,' she said, 'I've been so busy with my own troubles. I'll hear you read now.'

'It doesn't matter today,' I said. 'And I read the book all the way through. Won't you tell me what you'll do in London? I should like to hear about it.'

I had some small notion that if she talked I could perhaps twist her words a little so that she might see things differently and feel happier about going, yet God knows how anything I might say could help—unless it was that my world was so right that I felt I had the power to improve hers. 'Where will you stay?' I began.

'With my aunt in Bloomsbury.'

'You have cousins, too, in—Bloomsbury?'

'Three girls. Oh, and it's no use your saying it'll be pleasant for me. They despise me. They don't even like each other. They call me "Turnip" and hold their noses as if I've got dung on my boots. Not in front of my aunt, of course; when she's there we're all so sweet to each other it makes me ill.'

'No need to go to the theatre for a play-acting, then?'

She smiled at that. 'Oh, that's a very weak performance compared with some. You should see what happens when a young man calls. We all play cards—I *hate* cards—and we let him win, then tell him how clever he is and what a nimble brain he has. Isobel, the eldest, plays the pianoforte, and Sarah sticks out her chest and sings—some times I swear she'll split a seam. Elizabeth, who's tone-deaf anyway, just sits and smirks and says "yes" and "oh" and "la" and "how enchanting". Then, if the young man seems to favour one more than the others, the others must take care to be "unapproachable" as my aunt says. But afterwards, oh, Hester, you should see it . . . The one he's taken a fancy to is practically torn to pieces with words. And so is he. And that is life in Bloomsbury.

It's been like that for the past five years, and I have no reason to suppose that this year will be different. They're mad to marry. And I'm not.'

'It seems rather strange,' I said, squinting to thread a needle, 'that your aunt invites you to stay, considering that she has three daughters of her own to marry off.'

'Oh, she doesn't *ask* me to go. My mother arranges it. This year I think she must have bribed my aunt, and I believe it may have something to do with Dominic.'

'But I thought he was away. '

'So he is, but he'll be home shortly.' She flung herself across the bed, and I stabbed myself with the needle. 'Did I make you prick yourself? I'm sorry. Suck it. Oh, Hester, the boredom of it all. I won't be able to ride Honey, and I'll miss Sheba's puppies. The countryside's getting ready for summer and I won't be here . . . I'll be sitting in Bloomsbury, meek and weak, doing shell-work and embroidery. And I don't think there's a man living—much less a young and handsome one—who'll peep over my shoulder and admire *my* work.'

'No, he'd have to be blind,' I agreed, remembering the few times when she'd asked me to show her a stitch, 'for you handle a needle as if it were a dibble.'

'Now you're being insolent.' She rolled over on to her back and laughed. 'Somehow, though, it doesn't seem so bad now. Perhaps it *is* a little amusing—all that tarradiddle, that parade of false virtue—'

'Then try and laugh about it. After all, one day more is one day less. When will you come back?'

'In June.'

'Well, that's not long. My baby will be born in June I think.'

'I shall look forward to seeing it. I'd like to have lots of babies.'

'It would be best if you got a husband first.'

'Mmm, I suppose it would.'

'Then everyone will be happy.' I thought that then, at least, she'd be away from her mother and mistress in her own home. And there'd be babies for her; she needed children.

'I'm glad I have you to talk to,' she said. 'I could talk this way to my father, but of course it would only make him more miserable.'

'*Is* he miserable?'

'He'll miss me. If I could find a man like Father . . .'

'I'll miss you too,' I said.

Her life was so different from mine. My mother could make two potatoes, baked in the ashes of a winter fire, into a feast, shared in a kitchen warm with love. Lady Lindsey's voice whined across a carefully-laid table where candlelight swam in the silver dishes.

I thought of the way I'd married Matthew: because we were right for each other, because our furrows were drawn in the same pattern, and because we'd each seen in the other that thing that made me special to him and him to me. And because we couldn't put a word to it we called it love. Even though it wasn't the thing it had been (and that was largely my fault) it had been good at first . . . And I had Daniel and this coming baby. I hadn't had to paint a false picture of myself in order to find a husband. But then, I wasn't gentry.

The following day Miss Olivia left with her mother, Lady Lindsey's yapping dog, a hamper of food, several bottles of cinnamon water and the dress boxes chained to the back of the carriage. Her face under the lavender-coloured brim of her hat was hard and pinched, her expression sullen and resigned. Sir John kissed her as he handed her into the carriage, and for a moment her new face slipped, and she clung to him as if she would not let him go. Why *does* he let her go? I wondered, watching from an upstairs window, and then: but what else is there for her? If she stays here,

content only with him and the horses and dogs, she'll
end up in the Dower House, with her brother Dominic
as Squire in the Old Hall. That way she'll have nothing. This way is better—it gives her a chance, even
though she doesn't seem to want it.

The horses moved out, and the Squire turned back
into the house and shut himself in the library.

Mrs Broome decided that, in Lady Lindsey's absence, her room should be given a thorough turnout,
and Deb and Betty were working upstairs with a good
deal of giggling. There was a holiday air about the
house with her Ladyship away, and even Mrs Broome's
face seemed to have lifted a little. Polly had been set
to clean the kitchen cutlery—a job she hated, but she'd
sauced Mrs Hayes that morning, and Mrs Hayes could,
at times, be strict. Annie, who was suffering again with
her face-ache, had suddenly flopped on to a stool,
buried her head in her apron and started to cry. Mrs
Hayes, after telling Polly sharply to stop gawping, and
get on, poured Annie half a mug of gin and sent her off
to the blacksmith's to get the tooth drawn. 'That way
you'll be rid of the ache once and for all,' she said. So
when the Squire rang for tea, I was the only one there
to take it in.

He was sitting facing the window, only the top of
his head visible above the high-backed chair. I hesitated for a moment as he didn't move and, thinking he
may have been dozing, I set the tray on a side-table,
put the covered dish and the tea kettle on the hearth
and went out quietly.

An hour later, when I went to collect the tray, he
was leaning against the desk, idly twirling a big globe.
He looked up when I entered and stood, smiling at
me.

'It's Hester—isn't it?'

'Yes, sir. I've come for the tray.'

He nodded. 'How are you getting on here?'

'Oh, very well, thank you, sir.' Then, thinking I

might have sounded vain, went on: 'I mean, I like working here very much.'

'Olivia has spoken of you.' Then, suddenly: 'Do you know where you are?'

'Where I . . . ? Why, yes, sir, in Stoke Friary.'

He spun the globe. 'Just about—here.' He pointed to a black dot on what looked like a tea stain. I bent forward to see.

'Where is London?' I asked. He moved his finger a little. 'There? So close? Why, it's no distance at all.'

He laughed then. 'You're quite right, of course. The globe tells us that it's no distance at all.'

I picked up the tray and started to leave.

'It was thoughtful of you to set the dish on the hearth where it would keep warm.'

'I thought you were sleeping, sir.' I was confused because he was staring at me, and suddenly I couldn't meet his kind eyes. The room was unbearably hot, I couldn't catch my breath. It's the baby, I thought. Balancing the tray under my thumping heart I opened the door and went out.

The year moved towards summer. My seeds were sprouting: neat, feathery rows of carrots, pale rosettes of lettuce, darker potato leaves. During the long evenings I worked happily, heavily, with the hoe, and at the end of May, after making Mrs Hayes promise to let me know of any future casual work at the Old Hall —for I was now reluctant to leave the place for good—I collected my last wages.

I spent the few remaining weeks preparing for the baby, and one warm evening in late June I sent Matthew to fetch Alice Brackett, and I went up to bed. Later, when the sky beyond the window was black and the room bright and hot with two lamps and my own sweating body, Alice laid in my arms a tiny, perfect girl. The red, crumpled face had been wiped clean, but the dark hair—and there was such a lot of it—clung damply to the tiny skull. The eyes, smoky blue like a kitten's, stared at me, unseeing.

'Ain't she a little beauty?' Alice's face was a blurred shiny shape above me. 'What's to be her name?'

I looked again at the tiny head with the damp hair clinging in tiny scrolls, almost as if someone had practised writing the letter 'c' again and again. I thought of the spring afternoons up in the dark little bedroom at the Old Hall.

'Olivia,' I said, and slept.

TEN

It was good to be flat again: able to bend and reach easily, walk lightly. Good to watch the crimped red bud of my daughter's face open into the smooth, pale flower.

It was good to watch Daniel, now fifteen months old and sturdy, rock the crib, watching the baby's face and saying over and over again: 'Ssh, Livvy, ssh, Livvy.' And so she was known as 'Livvy'.

It was good to be working again in my own home, while beyond the window the patch of earth bloomed like a child's sampler, rows of neat stitches sewn in different shades of green. Soon my vegetables would be ready for lifting and marketing.

I had given a deal of thought to the means of getting them to market. There were only two possibilities and neither of them very good: I could bundle everything into a big net to be slung over my shoulder and carried into town. Daniel could stay with Alice Brackett while I was gone, but I would have to carry Livvy. Or I could ride in with the carrier. But it was well known that his old horse measured its paces between each inn from here to town and stopped obligingly at each one. I could see myself arriving late, the lettuces limp and wilted, and with stallholders and customers alike there before me, I could also see myself hauling back those same lettuces.

The matter was still in my mind one morning when I was spreading the children's linen to dry and saw the gaunt, yellow dog lying in the shade by the west wall

of Almongate. At first I thought he was dead. He
might well have been; his ribs showed like the staves
of a rotted boat, and the sinews of his legs were all
there was between hair and bone. I went towards him,
and he raised his head. He snarled, showing mean
teeth. His spirit hadn't shrunk with his flesh, and I
could not but admire his readiness for fight though his
weapons were weak. I backed away. His head lowered,
his eyes closed, and the flies settled again.

I had some broth hanging over the fire, and I ladled
a little into a bowl, broke in a crust and a rind of
cheese and placed it as near to the dog as I dared.
Then I went inside. Already an idea was growing in
my mind: he was a good, big dog and, properly fed
and if he were biddable, he would be able to pull a
small cart.

I collected the empty bowl and put out water. Later
I saw that the water had gone, and so had the dog. I
hoped he'd be back as I could ill spare the food. We
were still living tight for, until I could see a way of
adding to my savings, I was loth to let them dribble
away. Saving had become a habit, and each week I'd
find myself trimming the edges a little more. I was
growing mean. Matthew told me so. But if I had to risk
a few bowls of scraps in the hope of getting a dog to
pull a cart, then I must. I put out a piece of canvas
in the spot where I'd seen him, and the next morning
he was lying there.

I held out the bowl of oat-cake and skimmed milk
and waited, quite still. He eyed me warily, then got up,
stretching himself. He took a step forward and
stopped, but it was enough; he'd made the first move.
I watched from the window while he emptied the
bowl. He stayed close to Almongate for the rest of the
day and was asleep on the canvas at sunset.

I didn't tell Matthew of my plan. He showed little
interest in my doings except to warn me now and
then that I was riding too high a horse and so would
have further to fall. So I did my planning silently, and

the dog, I said, was hungry and thin and sick; I couldn't drive him away.

Some days later I put the bowl of food just inside the open door, and the dog, after trampling nervously back and forth outside, slunk in. I talked gently as he ate, then, when he'd finished, said: 'Here, boy.' He looked up, his ears twitched. I held out a hand and he came cautiously towards me. Suddenly he butted his head against my knee. I reached down and patted the harsh coat. For a moment we stayed like that, touching each other. And here, I thought triumphantly, was a horse I *could* handle, and not too high a one, either.

Later that afternoon I settled Daniel on my back, put Livvy in a basket along with a few freshly-dug vegetables and walked over to Alice Brackett's cottage.

'I've brought you a few bits,' I said, for Alice, having a large family, grew mostly potatoes. 'But I've really come to see Tommy. Is he at home? I've got a job for him.'

'He's outside. I'll call him.'

Tommy came in after taking off his clogs and leaving them outside. He was big for his thirteen years, and his face was lumpy and scarred from his falls for he took fits and so couldn't get regular work. He was neat handed with a piece of wood, though, and made small dishes and spoons and butter 'hands' which he sold, but he must do his whittling where his mother could keep an eye on him.

I told him what I wanted. 'A box,' I said, 'so high, and parted into spaces like a honeycomb, but square. Each space to hold something different: one for carrots, one for beans, and so on. Oh, and on the top I must have a kind of tray for lettuces so they won't crush. The box must be fitted with wheels and shafts and not be too heavy. Do you think you could do it?'

He was silent for a time, so I started again. 'A box—'

'A basket,' he said, his brow clearing.

'No, Tommy. Something much bigger than a basket

and parted into squares—like a lot of boxes joined together. To go on wheels.'

'Yes,' he said. 'Not heavy—so, a basket . . . A big
basket with strong frame and corners, and a tray on
top to fit on a peg and swing out, then you won't have
to lift it off to reach into the spaces below.' He ran outside and came back with a bit of stick and began to
draw in the sooty flakes of the fireback. 'Like that,'
he said, turning, his knobby face rosy with heat.

I bent and looked. 'Why—yes. You're a marvel,
Tommy. That's much better than the one I'd thought
of. Make it sound and strong. It must serve for many
journeys. I'll pay you two-pence an hour for a good
job.'

I walked back to Almongate well pleased with my
efforts. All that must be done now was to get the dog
used to walking in harness and obeying my word. I
started that very afternoon with a band of linen tied
under his chest. At first he didn't like it, ducking his
head this way and that and walking backwards trying
to free himself. But at last, finding he could not, he did
the sensible thing and got used to it. Then I tied two
strings to the harness and led him. It was a long job;
he whimpered and cried gustily at first, but after a
while he learned to respond to the reins.

At night when the children were in bed and Matthew at the Green Man I talked to the dog like a crazed
old woman. Now that my plans were made and I need
no longer contrive at this and that, time loitered. I was
missing the company of the servants at the Old Hall,
I think I would even have welcomed the sight of
Annie's sour face, and I was impatient for the years
to pass until Daniel and Livvy were of an age to sit
with me in the evenings. I was lonely.

It was the way of things, and it was natural, that
after a day's work a man should take his ale in a warm,
well-lit room where there was news and gossip, jokes
and a song, perhaps, just as it was the woman's way

to stay close to her hearth and sew or busy herself with household tasks in readiness for the next day. That, too, was natural and had always been the way. I *knew* it. Yet I felt—I *knew*—that there should be something beyond this.

I wished I'd asked Miss Olivia to lend me a book or set me some work. I pictured her in that little black speck on the Squire's yellow globe, then I was back in the library collecting the tea-tray, breathless in a room suddenly hot, unable to meet the look in Sir John's eye.

At such moments when this feeling came over me I'd go out to the well and dip myself a mug of water, drawing it in in a long, icy draught to steady myself, and I'd tell myself that all that was about me, the summer night, the dying fire pink through the window, the lamp spilling its light over the pile of sewing on the table, all these things were usual and familiar and right. They should have been enough and more than enough. And yet . . . with the night drawing a warm sheet over the land, the river dreaming silver in the distance, I knew a thirst that could not be slaked by the cold well-water. If I had words . . . I thought, groping desperately . . . If only I had learning enough to catch this feeling and wrap it in a word. Yet would a word have stemmed the feeling? Was any word big enough for that?

I'd thump the mug back on the shelf. 'You're getting mawkish, girl,' I'd tell myself, and I'd pick up my sewing and count my blessings.

By the middle of July a blanket of heat lay on the land that waited for rain, I worked slowly for the air was drained of freshness, and I was hot under my smock. I had made it in the style of those the carriers wore, it being equally good in fine or bad weather. It stood in its own shape away from me, and in wet weather turned off the rain like a sloping roof.

The village was still. There was no noise from the
forge. No birds sang, no blade of grass stirred, each
leaf was dawn clear and sharp and separate, very
brightly green against a slate sky. A slight breeze rattled the pear tree. I looked up, brushing my wrist
against my wet forehead. The rain must surely come
soon.

And at that moment I saw them: the Squire and
Miss Olivia cantering slowly up the lane. Miss Olivia
slid from her saddle as I picked up my skirts and ran
towards her, dropping a long bob as I reached her.

She raised me up. 'Do get up, Hester,' she laughed.
'You look like a large puff-ball.' She put her arms
round me. 'Oh, I *am* pleased to see you, and I've *lots*
to tell you. But when Father heard I was riding over to
see you he said he'd ride with me.'

We walked up the path, her arm round my waist. I
was only half listening to her, aware that, behind me,
walked Sir John. I felt his eyes on my back.

'You were right,' she was saying. 'This time I *did*
meet someone . . . I'm to be married.' She squeezed
me, and the dimple pricked her cheek. Her eyes shone
as if there was a light behind them. She was more
beautiful and more alive than anyone I'd ever known.
'And now—what of you? And the baby? Mrs Hayes said
it was a girl. I shall see her, of course? Is she pretty?'
Her voice raced breathlessly, and I laughed.

'She's pretty,' I said.

Miss Olivia turned. 'Come on, Father. You like
babies.'

I looked round. He was watching me. 'Please come
inside, sir,' I murmured, feeling the breath flutter in
my throat.

I took Livvy from the crib and laid her in Miss
Olivia's arms.

'Oh, sweet, sweet . . .' she crooned. 'What is her
name?'

'Olivia.'

'You—named her for me? Did you *really*? Oh . . . Father, did you hear?'

He nodded. I was aware of his strength and his gentleness, a strong presence in the familiar room. I turned quickly to straighten the cover on the crib while Miss Olivia paced up and down, chirruping at the baby. I would like to have said: 'Will you take a glass of wine?' I knew this was the way of things when gentry called, but my wines were newly-made and raw. Anyway, I had no glasses. Still, it seemed important that they—*he*—should know I was aware of such manners, so I said: 'I'm sorry I cannot offer you refreshment; my wines are not ready.'

'But your ale is,' Miss Olivia said, 'and I would welcome a mug. And I'm sure Father would. It's so hot.' She put Livvy back in the crib and stood rocking it gently with one foot. Daniel came out from the corner where he had retreated shyly and placed his foot beside hers, making the same movements and looking up at her. She took his hand.

'Your garden looks well,' Sir John said. 'You bought your seeds—your *good* seeds?'

I laughed, remembering the fierce, desperate tone in which I'd told him of my hopes on that January afternoon. 'Yes, I got them.'

'But *where* did you get *this*?' Miss Olivia pointed to the dog who came stalking into the kitchen and who had paused, one ear pointed ridiculously sideways.

'Oh, that's Manna. He came like a gift from Heaven.' I told them of the basket Tommy Brackett was making me and of my intention that the dog would pull it. I told them of my efforts to train the dog, and they laughed.

'And the reading, Hester? How is that progressing?'

'Well—' I shot a quick glance at the Squire.

'Oh, Father knows. He approves.'

'Then, to be truthful, it hasn't progressed. I haven't any books.'

'Oh, how stupid of me.' Miss Olivia beat her hands together. 'Of course you haven't. I didn't leave you any, did I? I'm sorry, but in the rush of going . . . And I wasn't very approachable, was I?'

'Well, I *have* been rather busy,' I reminded her.

'Indeed you have, what with gardens and babies and that remarkable dog. What breed would you say he was, Father?'

Sir John stared down at Manna who lay on his back waving his legs, jaw sagging in a foolish grin, and he touched his belly with a polished boot. 'I imagine his ancestors stopped asking themselves what *they* were generations ago.' He bent and fondled the dog's ear.

I watched Sir John's hand, remembering it soothing Saladin as we had talked in the lane that cold day, remembering it twirling the globe. Then I looked up at his face, and he was looking at me. 'The ale,' I said, bustling over to the corner shelf.

'But she mustn't let her reading lapse, must she, Father? I'll bring you a book or two. Tomorrow, perhaps. I'm going to be *so* busy . . . There is much I have to learn. And there'll be dressmakers . . . My brother, Dominic, is to be married, too. To Cousin Isobel—the one who plays the pianoforte.' She grimaced. 'But before then we are to have a grand ball at the Old Hall. See how I've changed? Once the very thought of one would have brought me out in a rash . . .'

She chattered on as she drank, then, as the gloom outside deepened, she put down her mug. 'Look at that sky, Father. We should leave now before the storm breaks. You know how thunder distresses Honey. Thank you, Hester, dear—' she kissed me. 'I'll ride by again, soon.'

I walked with them to the gate where their horses were tethered and stood watching until they turned out of the lane.

I sang as I rinsed the mugs. It hadn't mattered that they were thick and coarse, that there was only one cushion. They didn't care that it had been ale, not wine. None of it mattered at all. All the same, I thought, as I put the mugs away, I'll set aside the lettuce money until there is enough to buy three glasses —not the best, but not the cheapest either. Then, one day, I'd be able to serve them fittingly.

things would be so much nicer if I let myself

ELEVEN

Three times a week I walked into the town with Manna pulling the basket. When we reached my spot in the market I untied him, and he raced off to the Shambles, coming back some time later with a look on his face that told me he hadn't wasted his time.

For most of the day he lay quietly beside me, then, when I'd sold the last of my stuff, I harnessed him again, and we went home, Olivia lying in the empty lettuce tray and in my pocket a sugar twist for Daniel.

If Matthew were home before me the kettle would be singing over the fire. But only that. Sometimes, tired from the standing and the long walk, I wanted to say: Couldn't *you* have brought Daniel from Alice's? Couldn't you have set out the plates and mugs and bread? But I kept silent. If he had done any of these things it would have meant that he was, at last, a partner in my plans.

Once I patted my jingling pocket and said, cajolingly: 'I had a good day today.'

'Did you?' he said, without interest. 'I ripped my sleeve on the door nail; you might put a stitch in it.' And I felt that my day had been dashed to fragments. So, again, there were times when I thought perhaps it would be better if I gave up my hopes, worked in the house and made do, raising the children to be no better, to expect no more, than their parents. Thus things would be as Matthew wished. I lay sleepless

at night arguing with myself, until I remembered the
long walk to Stoke Friary, and that memory gave me
the answer: No! If you have a tool in your hands you
should learn to use it. So, as the weeks passed I stopped
speaking of the market to Matthew. I didn't tell him of
the women's chatter, nor of the fine carriages that
passed; of the coach that overturned as it thrashed
round a corner; of the meeting of the Mickletorn Jury,
of the day when the gypsies came, bright and ragged,
and played music that took me away from the market
and into a place so beautiful that, when they'd
finished, I found I was weeping. And, as Matthew
spent most evenings at the Green Man, it seemed
sometimes that we rarely spoke to each other at all.

Fortunately there was no market on the day of the
ball up at the Old Hall, so I was able to give a hand.
Mrs Hayes, true to her promise, had sent Jobey over
with the message that she'd be glad of some help, and
Mrs Broome had given permission for me to go.

The day had crept in through a pearly mist spiked
with the first faint frost that warns that, no matter how
blue the sky becomes, how warm the sun at noon, high
summer is past; the year has topped its crest and now
slides down towards winter.

The Old Hall was bursting with people. Anyone in
the village who had two hands and no job to put them
to had been found some sort of work. In one of the outhouses Tommy Brackett and two other boys plucked
capons in a sneezy snowstorm of feathers; in the
kitchen Mrs Hayes heaved herself from oven to table,
storeroom to sink, where Polly and one of the village
women plunged about in the earthy water, harvesting
an endless yield of washed vegetables. Over all hung
the good smell of cooking.

The Hall had been scoured and burnished; rooms
which had been shut up were aired and beds made up
for those guests who were to stay the night. In the
great hall each hanging drop of the chandeliers had
been washed, every gilt-framed mirror polished, the

floor was buffed to honeyed ice, and the whole lovely room shone. Only the flowers and greenery massed on the small side tables broke the sheen as they looked at themselves in yet another glossy surface.

Soon after eight the first carriages began to arrive, spilling their passengers at the front porch before sweeping on to the stables where Matthew and Jobey and the others were as busy as we were. There had been no time for us to eat, but Mrs Hayes had put some loaves and a cheese and a slab of fruitcake on the table and had told us to 'cut where you like, but no loitering.'

All the cold food had been arranged in the dining-room under Mrs Broome's supervision. And what food there was: enough, I thought, to feed the whole village. Fish had been brought upriver, there were pheasants sprouting fans of tail feathers, spiced eggs, fowls glazed with a sharp sauce, game pies and pasties, custards, jellies, tarts, sparkling bowls of syllabub, sweetmeats and sugared fruit, and across the table marched a row of tiny, porcelain boys each holding a basket of snippets to scent the breath.

The centre-piece was a cake made in the shape of a ship in honour of Miss Olivia's young man whose family owned a fleet of whalers in Yorkshire. The ropes and rigging were made of spun sugar, and a Frenchman had been brought from London to do it.

'And thank God he's gone,' Mrs Hayes said, as we rolled pastry. 'A right funny bogger he was. It was: "Pass me this, and hand me that," and so outlandish spoken you couldn't get his meaning. Had Polly in tears, he did, snapping his fingers and hissing like a goose . . . And you know Polly—it takes a lot to upset her—she's that brass-necked. He made us walk past his cake on tiptoe—*me*—with my joints as they are—in case all the sugar threads shattered. I never thought we'd get that creation into the dining-room in one piece, and my God was I glad when it was gone and so was he and I could walk easy again. A lot of playacting,

if you ask me—him and his little bag of tools and all.
Not but what it ain't the prettiest thing I've ever seen
. . . And I'm glad at last to see her Ladyship treating
Miss Olivia as if she was a proper person, bless her.'

Shortly after nine o'clock we in the kitchen found
ourselves moving more slowly, pausing to lean against
a table, to stop and speak instead of flinging words
into the air for anyone to catch. 'Now we can look to
ourselves,' Mrs Hayes said. 'My innards think I've been
strangulated.' She threaded three fowls on the spit
and put a great dish of potatoes into the side-oven. The
kitchen grew strangely quiet as if an unseen hand had
soothed it, and the first soft strains of music drifted in.
'Hark at that, now,' Mrs Hayes said, lifting a stubby
finger. 'Ain't that nice? We'll be having music while we
eat; what more could we want?'

Annie made a great pot of tea from the store of used
leaves and grudgingly pushed a mug across to me;
Deb, Betty and Polly pulled up stools to the table and
began to chatter. Mrs Hayes flopped into her chair by
the fire and was soon asleep, her lips gathering and
opening like a purse.

Presently I slipped from my stool near the window
and hurried up the back staircase. Although Miss
Olivia's young man had been staying at the Old Hall
for some days, and I had kept an eye open for them
riding by, I hadn't yet seen him. Now, perhaps, I might.

The stairs led into a small alcove at the end of the
gallery near where the musicians played. I stood
pressed against the wall—hidden, I thought—and the
sight below trapped the breath in my throat. Each
candle in the chandeliers bloomed like a crocus, each
crystal pendant held a rainbow; candles tipped the
wall sconces and the mirrors gave back their light.
And from wrists and throats, fingers and heads came
the brighter, harder glitter of jewels. Light shimmered
in the folds of silks and brocade, and laughter and talk
floated up to meet the music.

I couldn't see Miss Olivia from where I stood, but

Lady Lindsey and Sir John were standing at the end of the room talking to someone who, judging by her face, could only be Lady Lindsey's sister. Standing with them was a young man. Although his face was yellowish and puffy his hair was the same reddish-brown as Miss Olivia's. This, then, was Dominic. He was presently joined by a young lady—his cousin Isobel?—and as he turned to offer his arm his embroidered waistcoat strained across his rounded belly. Yes, he *did* have a look of Sir John, but whereas he should have been the fresher, finer one, and his father coarser, more used-looking, the opposite was true. As I watched he led the young lady towards the small room which had been set out with gaming tables.

The musicians struck up again, and in the middle of the room dancers were coming together like flowers in a posy. I stood watching, waiting for Miss Olivia to join them. At last she moved out from under the gallery where I stood, glowing in a saffron-coloured dress, and I leaned forward to look at the young man whose arm encircled her waist. He wasn't handsome or tall or elegant or dashing . . . But when he looked at her he was—beautiful. And she, tilting her face as though waiting for a kiss, wore that same look.

I should have left then, yet still I stayed, watching the drifting pattern of colour below until I suddenly realized that I was no longer alone. 'Isn't it—' I began, and turned, expecting to see one of the servants who had also come to peep.

'Isn't it—what?' Sir John asked.

The blood beat up my neck into my face. I swallowed. 'I'm sorry,' I whispered. 'I know I shouldn't be here . . . I just had to see . . . Miss Olivia . . .'

'Of course.' He didn't seem at all surprised. 'But you were saying—isn't it . . . what?'

'I don't know. Isn't it—well . . .' I lifted my hands helplessly. 'The music and the beautiful clothes, the colours, the sparkle . . . The—*spirit* . . . Isn't it—just *everything*.'

He was watching me steadily, a half-smile lifting his mouth. 'Indeed it is,' he said quietly. 'Everything.'

I found I couldn't look at him. I felt that his words held a hidden meaning. 'I must go now, Sir,' I said hastily. 'I know I shouldn't be here, but—' my voice trailed away as he moved to bar my way.

'Do you like to dance, Hester?'

'Oh, yes. But I've never danced like *that*, never with such grace.'

'Yet I believe you have exceptional grace.'

I was silent. Hot and breathless, I longed for the safe ordinariness of the kitchen with its warm familiar smells, where the girls sat with their elbows on the table, comfortably sipping. But he went on:

'Will you dance with me?' Then, seeing my horror: 'Oh, not down there, of course. I wouldn't put you to such confusion. No, here.'

He lifted the blue silk hangings that curtained off part of the end of the gallery. Behind was a large alcove lined with small-paned windows on three sides and a cushioned window seat below them. The dark curtains had, I guessed, been hung to show off more vividly the gold costumes of the musicians who played in front of them, and also to provide a sitting-out place behind.

'Well?' He was watching me. The light carved silver scallops in the silk of the lifted curtain.

'I couldn't, Sir,' I murmured. 'It wouldn't be—right.'

'Why not? Had you come to the servants' ball in January I should most certainly have claimed my dance with you, and it would have been perfectly—right.'

'But this is different.'

'How? There is music, there is dancing.' Then, after a moment: 'But you're right, of course. This *is* different. And I should very much like to dance with you, Hester. May I?'

His hand cradled my elbow, and the curtain dropped behind us, shutting us off from the rest of the world. The light from the hall below was sifted by the dark stuff, and the moon shone aslant through a side window, paving the floor with setts of pale light. He gently untied the knot of my apron, and it dropped like a tired ghost on a moonlit path.

He must have talked to me; he must have directed my steps, for there was his voice. But I don't remember the words. All I recall is his fine, thin face in the grey light. And even that is hazy for there are times when the body has no use for sight; only for being. It couldn't be possible for me to be stiff as an oak post while my bones melted, nor for a great brand to kindle me leaving no part unseared even as the goosebumps lifted on my arm. *One* of those things could happen or all of them at different times, but not all of them together. How can the body argue so with itself? Yet, with the unseen music playing and that strange half-light, I knew—and was—*all* of those things all in that time; and being so I ceased to be me.

At last the fiddle notes wavered along the air and were lost, and blindly I stooped and snatched up my apron, thrust aside the curtain and almost fell down the stairs.

'Come on, Hester, do,' Mrs Hayes said, as I reached the kitchen. 'Get sat in to the table or you won't get none of this good onion soup. Are you feeling all right?' She stopped with the ladle in mid-air. 'You're looking a bit flushed, girl.'

I took hold of myself, aware of the sickening smell of food. 'Yes. I'm just a little tired. I'll go now if I may.'

'Without eating first? An' we're having such a feast. You're loony,' Polly shouted.

'Run along then, duck. Come and see Mrs Broome for your money tomorrow.' Mrs Hayes turned to the big iron pot.

I lifted Livvy from the box in the corner where she'd spent the greater part of the day and went out into the cool night. The last notes of the fiddles played in my head; I would never forget their melody. I closed my eyes for a moment and saw again the grey light, the thin face. And I wished with all my heart that I hadn't crept up that back staircase. Now nothing would ever be the same again.

But that was foolishness, I knew. What fresh thing had *this* night brought? A man's whim, no more. And yet . . . I couldn't help thinking that a slight thread had linked me to him since that January day when I'd spoken to him for the first time. And—yes—even before that, when in the little hut by the bridge. Nancy, the old pedlar woman, had explained why it was kept in such state. Even then I felt my heart knew him; had I been high-born, with wealth and land, I like to think that I would have made a small shelter for those whose roofs were uncertain. And, had *he* been such a one, *he* would have rested in my shelter and blessed me, as I had him.

But it is one thing to have such thoughts and to hide them deeply, secretly, until with aching pleasure you allow a summer night to draw them out. It is another thing to think you see your own thoughts written in a man's eyes, think you feel them warm on his palm.

A gentleman's whim. No more than that.

As I turned into the lane I recalled seeing a dirty ragged boy eyeing the window of a pastry-cook's shop in town one day. A gentleman had stopped, tossed the boy a coin and passed on. The boy slipped quickly into the shop and came out cramming honey-cake into his mouth. I'd watched his face, a study in greed and joy, and I'd thought: Just for a moment, those two —the urchin and the gentleman—had made each other happy. Yet tomorrow the gentleman may not recognize the boy if he passes, and the boy will go hungry again.

And so it would be for me. These moments in the gallery were my honey-cake . . . Yet, when he'd repeated the word 'everything' there'd been something in his voice, his eyes . . .

With my thoughts tangled I held Livvy more close-

ly. Her fist sought my finger and curled round it. I
nuzzled her head against my breast, loving her fiercely, finding strange comfort in my thralldom to her.
And I almost laughed at myself for my fancies. Honey-
cake? Here, warm and real in my arms, was my bread.

TWELVE

But later, as I lay sleepless, my eyes fixed on the square of night sky beyond the window where a thin paring of moon hung, I saw in that dim light the same blue glimmer that had lit the gallery behind the curtains, and the notes of the fiddles still throbbed along my blood. Matthew snored gently beside me. And my mind turned and turned like a spit. What now, with everything changed, yet nothing different?

I pushed my face into the pillow; my shoulder blocked out the light. At last sleep came, thinly like a blanket worn in parts to show glimpses of what it covered; sleep brought dreams, and once I awoke to find my hand resting on the man beside me, only it wasn't Sir John as I had thought when I laid it there: it was Matthew. He grunted and turned over, leaving me alone with the question that came back and back. What now?

I thought again of the boy outside the pie-shop; there'd been nothing for *him* the next day, nor the next week: I'd seen him waiting, hoping . . .

I awoke the next morning heavy-eyed and went up to the Old Hall for my wages. I wanted to see Sir John, yet I knew that if I so much as caught a glimpse of him I would have hidden. So I was both glad and sorry to get back to Almongate, put the coins with my little hoard and throw myself into a frenzy of cleaning and scouring as if I were chasing devils from every crack.

Miss Olivia remembered her promise and rode over with the two books. She made me write a little and told me to practice. But I could see that she was restless and her thoughts were not with me. She strode up and down the kitchen, cuddling Livvy, talking to Daniel, then, all too soon, she hurried away. Her young man had gone back to Yorkshire, and now she was busy with plans for furnishing their house. I waited for her to speak of her father, but she didn't, and there was no way in which I could speak of him first.

My nights grew less troubled; my foolishness recognized itself for what it was. I hid the books from Matthew, taking them out after he had gone to the Green Man and the children were asleep, and I was alone with the noise of the fire and the wind outside, when the only movement was a piece of wood burning through and flaking in the grate, or the twitching dream-chases of Manna who lay across my feet.

Almongate was now less bare; there was another candlestick and more pans hung from the chimney beam. They were curtains, thick ones which kept out the draughts and made the kitchen a warm and cosy place.

I had read the first book and was beginning the second, but my interest wore thin, and I sat idly with it in my lap one night, watching the leaping flames drawn by the November wind in the chimney. I started when Manna growled. He looked at the door then moved forward. 'He's come,' I thought, and the sweet, fierce flame leaped within me. Impatiently I hauled Manna back by his scruff, told him to stay and snatched open the door. A figure leaned against the wall, bent as if in pain.

There was no mistaking the battered calash. 'Why, Nancy,' I exclaimed. Putting a hand under her elbow, I drew her inside. I pressed her into a chair and splashed some blackcurrant syrup into a mug, filling it up with hot water. I put a warm brick against her feet and hung my old cloak over her shoulders.

'Drink that,' I said, 'and don't talk.'

She sipped slowly, cupping the mug with cold, dirty hands. Then she said, hoarsely: 'He told me you were here. Tommy Brackett. He was holding a horse's head outside—'

'Hush. Don't talk. Tell me in the morning. You're going to bed now. A nice, warm bed. It'll be a long time since you slept in a bed, eh? Lean on me. We'll talk tomorrow.'

I kept up a stream of chatter, but I was shocked by her frailness. Before, when she'd spent the night with us in the hut, she'd been thin, but with a gaunt, whippy strength. Now she was a winter branch, brittle, sapless. I took Daniel from his mattress in the little room and laid him, still sleeping, on the bed I shared with Matthew. Then I helped Nancy down, put another hot brick against her side and left her.

The following morning she said she was a little better although her chest was 'tight as Granny's purse-strings,' and I persuaded her to rest for another day or so. She slept most of the time, eating very little, and on the fourth day she came down.

'A bit tottery, but I'm better now,' she croaked. 'Eh, I dunno what I'd have done if that Tommy Brackett hadn't told me where you was.'

'You're not thinking of moving on,' I said. 'The winter's here. Besides—' I had been going to say that she didn't *look* better.

'Nowt else for it,' she said, briskly. 'I've still got me bundle. I wear it wrapped around me now.' She tapped her ribs, and I remembered the piece of coarse stuff sewn with pockets to hold the laces and such that she peddled.

'Why not stay here?' I said. Then I wished I hadn't; what if Sir John came? But he wouldn't.

I made my voice a little warmer for I was ashamed, remembering how she'd shared her ale with me in the little hut, how she'd told Matthew of the work at the gravel hole. Had it not been for Nancy we wouldn't be in Almongate now. 'You *must* stay,' I urged. 'You once said you didn't fancy any more winters on the roads, and that was a year ago.'

'No more I do,' she retorted, 'but it's me life.'

'Well, stay until spring. You could keep an eye on the children for me while I'm busy.'

The old face was wistful. 'But how about the Mester?'

'Matthew? He won't mind. If it hadn't been for you we wouldn't have stayed on here those few days and then he wouldn't have got his job in the stables.'

'Aye. I heard about that. A right stroke of luck it was . . . Then I *will* stay. Just until spring. And I'm obleeged to you,' she added, royally.

With Nancy to give an eye to the children I was free to work in the garden, and all that November Tommy Brackett and I dug and dug, clearing more ground. I'd be working a bigger piece next year and growing more, and on fine days when my breath smoked off into the crisp air and the spade bit cleanly into the earth the rhythm of my movements lulled me into a feeling of absolute peace. Each clod of earth I lifted nursed tiny lives that breathed and coupled and died in the dark; each crumb of soil cradled unseen seeds with a mesh of spent roots. Each spadeful was a small, separate world to be linked with the next at planting time, to become part of the greater earth that would be green in the summer. And, as always, the thought of the land, the smell and feel of it, the glimpses of the life within it, brought a sense of belonging. I was part of the earth, just as the earthy cracks of my hands were part of me.

I'd think of the chicks I'd get in the spring, and the pen Tommy was to make: I wasn't going to lose any eggs by the fowls laying away, nor was I going to take any chances of having them stolen when they wandered off through the hedge. I'd been promised a piglet, too.

And, at the end of those days, when my back ached and my hands seemed curled to the shape of the spade haft, and I was almost too tired to eat the meal Nancy had prepared, I'd sleep deeply, thinking only for a small time of a hand cupping my elbow beneath an upswept curtain. And in that last little moment, just before sleep, I remembered the sweetness of it, remembered it as something beautiful which had happened and gone—like a happy day that was past.

In those weeks I grew to love Nancy. She talked a lot, and her words were worth hearing. Some of the things she told me in truth could have been lifted straight from a tale. Like many old people she remembered things long gone more clearly than recent events, and I stored up her stories to tell the children when they were older.

As Christmas drew near I decided that ours should be a merry one, so I dug into my savings for the things that would help make it so. For Matthew I bought a blue woollen waistcoat; I got Tommy to make a wooden rattle for Livvy, and for Daniel I made a dog out of some yellow cloth, using Manna as my pattern. I bought a length of red flannel, and I asked Alice Brackett to make it up into a petticoat for Nancy and to sew some true lovers' knots round the hem. I wanted it to be a surprise on Christmas morning. And it was.

'Eh, I've never had such a one as this since I were a bride,' she said, and she put it on on top of her dress. Later, in the evening, drunk with the day's delight and the quantities of ale she'd taken, she hoisted her skirts, and kicking up her feet she sang in her cracked old voice: 'Wah Willum wedded Winifred's wench' and 'O promise me in May' and other songs that were new to us. Daniel banged Livvy's rattle on the table, Manna barked, and Livvy chewed the yellow dog's ear into a matted pulp. We sang all the old Christmas songs and roasted chestnuts and bobbed for apples. Matthew too caught the feeling and took hold of my waist, dancing

me round the room. The green bough hanging on the
chimney gave off a cool, fresh scent. It was the best
Christmas we'd known.

'You'll have to help me upstairs, gel,' Nancy said at
last, trying to pin up her tumbling hair and only
succeeding in looking even more wild. 'I'll never manage them on me own.' So, with Matthew leading and
me supporting her from the back, we got her on to
her mattress. 'Eh, it's been a right merry day, and
you're a rum lass,' she said. 'I love you like you wuz
me own daughter, so give us a kiss before me 'ead
spins off.'

Nancy was still with us that day in spring when Miss
Olivia was married. Most of the village turned out to
see her ride away with her bridegroom.

'She's a good 'un,' Nancy said, waving stick-like arms
as they bowled away. 'Puts me in mind of you, somehow. Not that you look alike, you so dark and her
tawny-red, but there's sommat . . .'

'I hope she'll be happy,' I said, fervently, as we
walked slowly home. I shifted Livvy in my arms so that
I could take Daniel's hand, but he preferred to cling to
Nancy's skirts. 'I grew fond of her, and I'll miss her.'

'Everyone will,' Nancy said, 'barring her mother.
But then she's been queer ever since she realized about
Master Roland being a bit wanting. She wouldn't believe it at first, you know. She blamed the nurse that he
didn't walk when he should and couldn't speak a clear
word at four years old. So she sent that nurse packing
and got another; then, when that one couldn't do
nowt, she sent *her* off. That lad's had more nurses than
I've got toes. But then, at last, her Ladyship couldn't
do owt else but admit he was loony. 'Til then she
doted on him. Now she can't abide the sight of him,
and it's all Dominic now. You'd feel sorry for her,
really—only no one does any more. And how that dear,
kind man could—'

'How do you know all this? About Lady Lindsey?'

'Oh, I hear bits here and there. And don't forget I've been coming through this place for the last thirty years. I've seen young folks grow old and old folk die. I never liked that Dominic myself,' she said, her mind jumping back, 'not even when he was a child and a sight prettier than he is now. He wasn't like a bain, somehow—he was crafty and sly and cruel. And now he fair gives me the creeps, and I'm not a fanciful woman. God help Stoke Friary when he inherits.' She looked at me keenly. 'Rents'll go up on all his property, and he won't bother hisself keeping up the hut by the bridge. Things'll change here, and not for the better.'

'What a gloomy picture you paint,' I said. 'Perhaps he'll be different now that he's married.'

'Aye, and pigs might fly,' she laughed, 'but I shan't be here to see 'em. Now come on, *do*—it'll rain before long.'

'I could never understand why Lady Lindsey disliked Miss Olivia,' I said, as we reached the gate. 'I mean—it's not like a mother—'

'She's jealous, I'd say. I suppose with Master Roland not being what he ought, then Miss Olivia favouring her father like she was his pet hound—well, I expect her Ladyship got sour. If she had troubles and misery perhaps she could bear them better if she passed a bit on, like. That's the way some folk are. And gentry are folk when all's said and done. We've got a saying where I come from: "There's nowt so funny as folk".'

Two weeks later, a sudden heavy shower put a brief stop to my outside work, and I went into the house to find Nancy lying on the floor by the table. I got her upstairs, but one side of her body dragged limply, and her face had slipped like a jelly set in a tilted mould. Only her eyes were alive as I laid her down.

Her good arm groped towards the pillow, but even that little movement seemed too much for her. I raised her head and shook up the pillow, thinking that was what she wanted. Still her hand searched and her eyes tried to speak. Then I realized she was trying to reach her pack; it was all she had in the world; it was her past and her future—her one certainty. A few days ago she had spoken of taking to the roads again. I rolled the pack, tied the tapes and closed her hand over it.

For the next few days she seemed to sleep, stirring only when I moistened her lips with herb brew or placed a fresh mat of moss and straw beneath her to keep her clean. Her eyes had sunk back into her head, and she hardly moved.

One afternoon I sat with her, singing 'O promise me in May', but there was no way of knowing whether or not she heard. The world outside was fresh and green and full of promise, but I knew there would be no May for Nancy. I was watching her die. The tears choked me so that I could no longer sing, and just for a moment her eyes seemed to look at me, to smile, as if she understood and was telling me not to sorrow. Her hand trembled within mine. Her breathing was fast as if she'd been running for a long time, and the fluid inside bubbled with every breath. Her cracked, bluish lips moved a little as if trying to shape a word, and I realized she was giving me the canvas pack.

I took it from where it lay, clamped to her side by her powerless arm, and said: 'For me?' My voice, though a whisper, was loud in the stillness. She seemed to smile then, the message left her eyes, and the lids closed, gently as a daisy at dusk. They would not open again in Almongate.

The house was hollow, the nights by the fire dull without Nancy's salty talk, and I slipped back into my earlier pattern of passing my evenings with only my thoughts for company.

About a week later, having put the children to bed, I took up the sheet I was making for Livvy's crib. Mrs Rowson at the Green Man had given me two pieces of linen which I was joining together, and I thought I would put an inset of narrow lace at the join; it would

SO WILD A LOVE   125

prolong the job and eat away a little more of the
lonely time.

I took Nancy's pack from the cupboard and unrolled
the stiff canvas, noting—as I had when I had taken it
from her—the heaviness along the bottom edge. I knew
that the few loops of ribbon, laces, the combs and
pins could not weigh so much, so, taking my scissors,
I unpicked the stitches of the tiny pockets cunningly
hidden within the larger ones. From each of them I
took a coin. Eight guineas in all.

I'd thought all my tears were spent while I washed
the still face and wiped the last trickle of moisture
from her chin and plaited the hair into two thin cords.
But now I stood with the weight of her life's savings
in my hand, recalling the threadbare green-black rags
that hung about her; the boots, clumped and cobbled
and patched, the calash she was so proud of and I
thought of the warm, quilted cloak she might have
had, the good strong boots—and I wept again.

THIRTEEN

Summer came, frothing the roadsides with cow parsley, trailing old man's beard over the hedges. By the river sow thistle, ragwort and tansy shone yellow in the sun, and in my garden the onions and potatoes swelled, the currant bushes were hung with ripening beads, and the pig fattened. I now had a few steady customers at my garden stall, and I called regularly with my vegetables at five houses on the way into town.

Each week the children seemed to grow; Daniel to find a new word, a new game; each day he looked a little more like Matthew. And Livvy, now one year old, was into everything, constantly crooning in a surprisingly deep, husky voice, occasionally stopping to look at me and say "Mam-mam," then laughing at her own cleverness. I looked forward to the evenings when we played together, when I could watch them and hold them. I enjoyed my children.

So there was little time for thinking of those things that lay confused in my mind, or of that girl who, seemingly years ago, had danced in a moonlit alcove and known . . . what? But sometimes, during my quiet minutes in the late afternoon, my thoughts chased after the old dream until it filled the moments and crowded out the more sensible business of everyday living.

With Miss Olivia in Yorkshire and Mrs Hayes not needing my help, for life at the Old Hall was quiet now, I sometimes felt that my ties with the family there were broken. Then Master Roland would pass with Miss Goodbody on their way to the river. He always stopped to shout and wave, and I'd take him a gingerbread man from the jar I kept for the children. He had remembered the little custom we followed: first my touch on his cheek, then the kiss. I wondered if I were the only person allowed to kiss him. According to Miss Olivia, I was. 'You've charmed him, Hester,' she'd once said. 'He screams and stamps if I so much as touch him.' But he was always gentle with me, and sometimes I'd bring him into the garden and he'd watch the fowls and jerk himself about in mimicry until I ached with laughing.

Sometimes Matthew came home talking of the horses that were being stabled at the Hall, so I'd know that there were visitors. I'd question him, try to draw him into conversation, but as soon as the evening meal was done he'd take his coat and go out. Those were lonely evenings, and on this particular night he had hardly spoken.

At last, sick of my own gloom, I peeped at the two sleeping children, folded the sewing I had finished and took it round to the Green Man. I stood by the kitchen table while Mrs Rowson inspected my stitches. The half-open door led into a passage between the kitchen and the tap-room. It was a warm night, and the door to the tap-room was propped open. I could see beyond, to where Matthew leaned against the counter talking to the girl who drew the ale. I recognized by the back of her marigold-coloured head a pretty, rather slow-witted girl from outside the village. I also saw, from the set of her shoulders, that one arm rested on the counter. And I guessed from Matthew's face that he was touching it.

Shocked, I drew back quickly before he could look up and see me watching. And I thought in that moment how marriage can change a man. Before we were wed it had taken all Matthew's courage to *look* at me, for he hadn't spent his earlier years learning the way with girls. But now marriage had given him that knowledge, that . . . ease, and the differences which had lately grown between us had sent him to use it elsewhere.

I could blame myself in part, but not wholly, for what I did I did for *all* of us, Matthew, Daniel, Livvy and myself. If he lost his job it wouldn't be the hard blow it could have been. But I hadn't seen that in following my own ambition, I had set Matthew free.

And so, when in those warm summer nights he reached for me, I quelled any bitter thoughts and answered his need as a friend who shares the same need, the same hunger, and—in the same way—feels cheated that it can be only partly satisfied. And perhaps, in that small, strange way which I didn't fully understand, we were closer to each other at those moments than at any other time in Almongate. And yet, I envied him: he, at least, saw and spoke to his love.

But . . . I had my work. Once I thought it would be enough. Now I must make it so.

On a fair afternoon in mid-October I was hanging the freshly washed curtains. Spring had been too busy a time to attend to the indoor jobs, and all summer the sun had pried the window, pointing accusingly to the dirty patch along the wall where Manna rubbed himself, and the small, damp stain against the chimney. Today, I decided I would put the house to rights for soon I would be busy in the garden.

There were so few of those days—just a handful between Michaelmas and All Hallows—when the trees hold their bright leaves a little longer, when the morning air is thin and crisp, and the sun, less thirsty, leaves the dew on the grass: the most beautiful time of the year, and the saddest. So short a season.

I was twitching the curtains into place when I heard the steady drop of hooves outside. As they stopped I bent to peer through the window, then I jumped from the stool and opened the door as Miss Olivia slid from the saddle.

She'd changed. She was thinner and more elegant.

Her blue velvet habit was well-cut and uncreased, and the little matching hat sat pertly over one eye, its feather curving to follow the line of her cheek. What her mother's scoldings hadn't wrought love had.

She came smoothly up the path, then, nearing me, gave the little darting movement of the untidy, impetuous, lovable girl I'd known. She took both my hands in a warm clasp and kissed me, and her movements stirred the fragrance in her clothes.

'Hester,' she exclaimed. 'And Daniel, handsome Daniel, and Livvy. But how they've *grown*.' Daniel hid behind my skirts in a fit of shyness, and Miss Olivia lured him out with a small toy which she took from the purse that swung from her waist. Then she stood looking round the room, smiling.

'Please sit,' I said, politely. Then: 'Oh, it *is* good to see you again. And you look so elegant.' As I spoke I went over to the cupboard and took down a bottle of cowslip wine and two of my new glasses.

'Mmm,' she murmured, holding the glass up to the light. 'This is rather nice. Are you very rich, Hester? Tell me, do you make a fortune with your garden stall?'

'Of course,' I said, matching her mood. 'Almost five guineas every market day. I shall buy a gig and a fine, big horse like Saladin. Look at my gown—can't you see I'm wealthy?'

She giggled into her glass, then set it down and lifted off her hat, shaking loose her bright, curly hair. She smiled a wide, girlish grin, and I grinned back.

'Oh, it's good to be back here.' She took Livvy on her lap and gently stroked the dark, silky hair. 'My husband wanted to try out a new harpoon—that's what they use for catching whales, you know—so he's gone on a little trip, and I'm *here* on a little trip. Whaling is terribly dangerous, but he insisted on going with them, and if I were at home I'd be gnawing my nails imagining all kinds of terrible things. So I thought I'd come here and see Father.'

'I miss you,' I said, abruptly.

'Do you, Hester? Do you really?'

'You don't know . . . Sometimes I think that everything that happened, the reading and the talks we had —well . . . I know they happened, but with you gone I often think that those days belonged to a different life. Only when Roland comes by do I feel that there is something left from those other days. Once I felt a part of the Old Hall . . . Silly of me. I was only a servant. But now . . .'

'Yes? Now?'

'It's gone,' I said, flatly. 'This—' I waved my hand— 'is all my life now. And much as I love Almongate, sometimes I want to kick the walls down. My life stopped growing when you left, and there's no one to teach me things now. But tell me of yourself. Is all well in Yorkshire?' I wished I'd noticed Yorkshire on the Squire's globe, for I had no idea where it lay.

'Oh, I like it. There are winds—great, scouring winds that come ripping in off the sea and make riding an adventure. And the river—so wide. Hester, much, much wider than the Trent or the Thames, and the smacks go beating out with their brown sails curved. Sometimes I'm riding on the very rim of the world—at least that's how it feels. It's because of being near to the sea, I suppose.'

'I've never seen the sea.'

'You'd love it. I do. Sometimes, when I watch the barges coming downriver I think: Have you passed Almongate? Did you see Hester and that beautiful little poppet, the baby Olivia?' She held Livvy high above her head, and the baby laughed. 'And I think: Did I see you years ago, old barge, when as a child I used to creep up to the servants' bedrooms at the Old Hall and stand on a stool so that I might watch the boats in the distance? So you see, Hester, the river still ties me to Stoke Friary.'

I filled up her glass and took a deep breath. 'How—

how is Sir John? He used to ride by sometimes, but I haven't seen him since—'

'The night of the ball?'

'You knew?'

'I saw you,' she said. 'In the gallery, and you went through the curtains together.'

'We danced,' I said in a low voice.

'Of course you did. Did you suppose I thought otherwise? Oh, Hester. Shame. I know my father and, I think, I know you.' We were both silent for a moment, then she went on: 'You know, happiness and love sharpen the senses, heighten one's perception. Being so unbelievably happy myself, I wish others to be happy. Particularly my father. He has so little, really, and with me gone . . . He *deserves* happiness,' she said, fiercely. 'So I thought when I saw you together—' After a while she went on: 'He is a good man, but like many other good men he is not always appreciated, and very rarely understood—particularly by his own kind. Some say he's a radical. He's *human*— that's all. But to be human is to be suspect. He pays better wages than most, and that makes him unpopular with the landowners. They say it encourages the labourers to set too high a value on their labour; that it breeds unrest—even revolution. Fools—it's their own attitude that breeds *that* . . . iron-fisted autocrats to whom possession is all.'

I sipped my wine. 'I don't understand much about such things,' I said at last.

She laughed. 'Nor do I, really. And the less we understand, the better, I sometimes think. But . . . he's lonely. Oh, yes, Hester, one can be as lonely at the Old Hall as another can be in Almongate.'

I blushed that she could read my thoughts so easily.

She continued: 'When I was teaching you to read he sometimes asked how you progressed. I thought he wanted to know what kind of teacher I was. Later, I realized that that was not the reason he asked.'

I sat foolishly pleating my apron between finger

and thumb, wishing we could have done with this talk, but, at the same time wanting to hear more.

'I often wished he'd taken a mistress. Most men would. Someone pretty and witty—or maybe only pretty and . . . grateful. Then, when my mother had one of her tantrums, or Dominic became more un-bearable than usual, Father could have ridden off to some little house in town and restored himself. But I talk nonsense. He has no mistress. And, you know, that's rather odd in my family. My great-uncle Nicholas had several mistresses, all at the same time. It is said that he taught one of them the language of the gutter to . . . enhance their loving. If one can call it "loving".' She shuddered, then looked at me, thought-fully. 'Father always said that you have a smile that spreads happiness beyond your face to the person you're with. Why, Hester, you're blushing!'

'And wouldn't you?' I retorted, rudely.

She put Livvy down and came over to me, laying a hand on my shoulder. 'Don't be cross, Hester, dear. I love my father very much. I would like him to be happy. That night when he came to you on the gal-lery and looked at you as he lifted the curtain, he was . . . I've never seen him look quite like that, and I knew, or I thought I knew—'

'What?'

She lifted her shoulders helplessly. Something about her, the way she held her head, brought back the pic-ture of him as I'd first seen him, sitting high above me on Saladin—his kind face, steady eyes, the half-smile, the hands, slightly curved, as they caressed the horse's neck. I looked down at my own hands, still unthinkingly rucking the limp cotton of my apron. Rough and red, etched by the earth, pricked by the needles of a thousand stitches, dry—almost scaly. I thrust them out of sight beneath my apron.

Miss Olivia lowered her hat on to her curls. 'I must go now. Thank you for the wine. Thank you for listen-ing to me.' She leaned forward and kissed me, hugged

Livvy, wiped some crumbs from Daniel's mouth with a wisp of handkerchief which freed that same fragrance as did all her movements, now.

I watched her ride away, urging the mare to a gallop so that her curls bounced against her shoulders. She waved as she turned out of the lane, and I went back into the house.

In the scrap of mirror I studied my reflection. I expected, somehow, to look different. Hadn't she been trying to tell me something? I ought to look different because I knew, now, that my fancies hadn't been fathered by my own desires. But, beyond a certain sadness in my eyes and a droop of the mouth, the dim glass gave back my everyday face.

I tilted my head to one side and pursed my lips into the small smile of the fashionable ladies, but I looked like a fowl; I shook out my hair and piled it, haphazardly, on to the top of my head, trying to achieve the frizzled, cloudy shape that was fashionable, and succeeded only in looking even more like a fowl, a long-necked rooster that perches with his tail in the wind.

I laughed out loud at my efforts and spun round, running my eyes over the room, trying to see Almongate through *his* eyes: a cottage with a low-beamed ceiling and a window set a little askew, and only the barest of furnishings. Outside, the garden lay neat and dying. Nothing more. It was for use not beauty.

I'll plant roses, I thought, excitedly. Four bushes at each side of the gate and a yellow one beneath the window. I saw my dress with critical eyes: faded print, the colours almost lost across the shoulders where the sun had bleached it, torn many times beneath the arms and patched with strips cut from the hem, little scraps whose brightness showed what the whole had once been. When? Five, six years ago?

My thoughts filled the room—tiny, beating wings that echoed my flurried heart-beats. There was the money from Nancy. I would lay a little aside for the

children, and I'd get a new dress of a soft, warm,
honey-coloured wool: nothing elaborate for I wasn't
the kind for fripperies, but I'd have a little lace somewhere—yes, a fall of creamy lace at the neck. And ear-
bobs, too—amber ones to suit the dress. And shoes, of
course, dainty shoes with coloured heels, though
doubtless I'd have to learn to walk gracefully in them.

Oh, yes, I would do these things. If he wanted me
I must be fit for him. I would try and be beautiful for
him.

I took Daniel on my knee, and he placed his hands
at each side of my face and squeezed. I laughed and
he laughed, and in that moment it seemed that there
could be no happier person in the whole of the world.

FOURTEEN

Matthew spooned the last of his porridge into his mouth and scraped back his stool. 'I'm off then,' he said, reaching for his coat. 'Squire's sold Velvet—I got to take her over to Miston Magna today. Anything you want while I'm passing through town?'

'I can't think of anything,' I said.

'Not even a pair of them fancy gloves?' The words were spoken lightly, but I felt my face go pink. So my little attentions to my hands hadn't gone unnoticed.

'I doubt I'd have much use for them. Besides,' I teased, 'if you're thinking of spending that kind of money I ought to be along with you to make sure they fit.'

'Oh, it wasn't *my* money I was thinking of spending,' he said, wryly. One more little tap to knock the nail home, but I let it pass and helped him on with his coat. And he said no more.

It was a day much the same as any other, and when Matthew didn't come home at the usual time I guessed he'd been delayed on some errand so I ate my supper, dishing his and setting it on the hearth to keep warm. Then, in the usual order of my evenings, I put the children to bed, drew the curtains and took up my sewing. I'd bought some very fine stuff from the mercer's to make handkerchiefs which, doubtless, would earn me another dose of Matthew's views about getting above myself.

My fingers, still a little rough, rasped on the material like teasels, setting my teeth on edge, and when Manna's throaty growls warned me of someone coming up the path I was glad to put aside my work and go to the door.

The man standing there was a stranger, but he stepped right past me, closing the door behind him. 'It's about Matthew,' he said. He'd been running.

'Are you from the stables?' I asked.

'No. Though I sometimes work at the Old Hall. I'm Jack Hallam.'

Where had I heard the name? Of course—I remembered: Annie's young man, the man who might now have been her husband had we not come to Almongate. I waited while he stared levelly down at me. He had a good face, I thought, neat and plain, with even, well-formed features.

'Yes? About Matthew?'

There was a strange wariness in his eyes now, and something else . . . pity?

'Where is he?' I asked sharply.

'There's been an accident.'

'How? Where? What kind of accident?'

'He took a horse over to—'

'Yes, yes, I know all that.'

'I met him afterwards in the town, and we went up to the Fleece for a drink. When we were crossing the market-place on the way back there was a crowd gathering—stockingers, mostly. They were going down to the Bottoms—'

'What's all this to do with Matthew? Tell me. I don't want to know about the stockingers. For God's sake tell me *now. Where is he?*'

'He's at a house back of Bone Lane. I—we were in the market-place like I said, and we got shoved about a bit, there was a bit of a crush, and we tried to walk round 'em. I reckon Matthew slipped in some muck or sommat, anyway his feet went from under him, and he caught his head a great clout on the edge of a mounting-block. But he got *up* . . . A bit dazed, like, but he *seemed* all right . . . His head was bleeding, but

I thought . . . He took my arm for a step or two. Then he went down. So I got him to this house—it's my mother's cousin's. He's—I'm sorry, Missus, he's—'

'Dead.' I read in his face the word he couldn't say.

He nodded, wiping his mouth, and I stood frozen thinking: This isn't true, his supper's there waiting . . . This isn't happening.

'I'll take you to him,' he said, gently.

'No.' I plucked my cloak from its peg. 'Just tell me where to find him and I'll go alone.' My voice came from a long way off, like an echo thrown back. 'If you'll help me get the children down to Alice Brackett's I'd be obliged. She'll have them while I'm gone.'

'Now, Missus, you can't go into town alone. Any time it'd be bad enough, but tonight there's likely trouble.'

'I'll have the dog,' I said, slipping the leather loop over Manna's head. 'Here, you carry Daniel, and I'll take Livvy.'

He stood for a moment, undecided. I had the feeling that he expected me to faint, to fall weeping into a chair. He wasn't prepared for this brittle frost. I wanted him gone. I wanted to be alone. 'Come on,' I said, opening the door.

'I'm sorry,' he said again, awkwardly. 'I've had a hand in a few things—lost my job on a farm 'cos they said I was a bloody firebrand . . .'

I was half-way along the path, hauling Manna back as he strained forward into the darkness. 'Come on,' I flung over my shoulder.

'You'd better let me go in with you,' he said again, after I'd turned abruptly away from Alice's soft, pitying eyes. 'There were rumours that they were going frame-breaking, and likely the Militia will be—'

'I'll go *alone*.' I almost shouted. Then: 'But I thank you for offering. I'll be quite safe with the dog.'

'We-ell, if that's what you . . . I'll just walk with you as far as the Green Man, then.'

In an hour the whole of the village would know

about Matthew, I thought. In about one minute, or as
long a time as it takes to draw a mug of ale, that
orange-haired girl will know that he'll never again
lean on that counter, look into her eyes, never touch
her arm again.

I found the narrow little house in the lower side of
town, without difficulty. The woman who answered
my knock expected me; she lighted me silently up to a
room beneath the roof where Matthew lay on the floor
beside a stocking-frame. She left the lamp with me,
and I set it by his head. It shone on the dark, ruffled
hair, rusty with dried blood above one ear and streaked
with something paler. Manna darted forward to flap
his tongue over Matthew's face, and I pulled him back,
sickened.

I lifted Matthew's shoulders and held his face
against my breast. So still; so very still. None of the
slow dawning of expression that was Matthew. It was
as if the candle had burned out in an All Hallows' Eve
lantern, leaving an empty meaningless mask cut in the
pattern of a face. An empty face. Not the boy's face
that had shone shy and heartbreakingly happy beneath
the hawthorns at Saxtoft that long-ago spring when we
spoke of marriage. Nor the proud face at my bedside
when Daniel was born. Nor the face alight with excitement at having ridden Saladin from Blue Spinney
to the Old Hall almost two years ago . . . Now the
face was quiet, the chin no longer jutting in his dis-
approval of me as it had so many times in the past two
years, even on this very morning.

I gently laid him back on the floor and called to the
woman for some water and a cloth. Then I slowly
bathed his face, smoothed his hair and knelt beside
him for a while, my fingers tracing the bones of his
temples and cheek down to the jaw. I kissed the cold,
quiet lips and rose stiffly, suddenly old, and left him to
his darkness.

Downstairs the woman waited, and I handed her the

lamp. 'When will he—when will they come for him?' she whispered.

'Tomorrow,' I told her. 'I'll see to it.'

The light showed the relief on her face. 'I'm sorry,' she murmured, 'it's just that that frame up there is our living—and with him lying there I couldn't . . .'

'Tomorrow,' I repeated, pressing a shilling into her hand. Then I went out.

The market-place was almost empty. The dim lamps hung like tired moons among the elms. A bent figure groped in the rubbish piled at the steps of the Malt Cross. A thin dog sniffed after Manna, lifted its leg against a tree and wandered off. I could hear a violin being played somewhere, and over to my left voices, muted by distance. The frame-breakers or the Militia, perhaps, but I didn't care.

From the roof of the Exchange the faint stone shape that was the Goddess of Justice looked down over the town. In sudden frenzy I shook my fist at her and swore. If Matthew had to die, why could it not have been on the stones of the stableyard, near the earth, the soil, the smell of leather and horses—the things that mattered so much to him. Not on the littered cobbles of a town he didn't care for, felled because of a struggle that meant nothing to him.

I went out of the market-place, past the inns, up the hill and alongside the town fields, leaving the weak lamplight behind. And as the rough road unravelled beneath my feet my thoughts unrolled like a spool of thread that cannot be stopped, recalling images of Matthew and happier times we had shared.

The road twisted. Ahead the windows of a great house shone like topaz. To my left the river ran, dark and silver. A scattering of stars winked coldly, the same stars that had shone on Matthew when he walked home from the Green Man. Now, as they glittered, they mocked. 'He's dead,' they said. 'He's gone. What matter? Come what will we shall be here.'

The same wailing wind pounced on me as I turned into the lane, plucking persistently at my cloak. That wind and those stars would be there when I, too, was dead; when all my feeble strivings had come to fruit or had withered. And what, in the long reach of years, did any of it matter? Hester Calladine, so small—who was she?

My head was bowed against the wind, and my hood had slipped forward, almost covering my eyes, but I knew the way as a blind man knows, and steeped in my despair I didn't notice the pink glow behind the curtains of Almongate.

I opened the door and was dashed awake. For a moment I thought I had come to the wrong cottage. The fire which should have been dead flamed high, chasing shadows round the room and making a safe, rosy cave of the little space round the hearth. The table had been pulled up to the fire, and the flamelight washed round the curve of the bottle, glowed on the waxy oranges. There was a cold roast partridge and some polished, red apples. And there was Sir John waiting for me.

He didn't speak, just drew me into the warmth, gently pushing me into the chair warm from his own body. He laid his coat over my shaking shoulders and slipped off my shoes, kneeling to chafe my feet with gentle hands. I sat without will, without ableness or self, racked by long shudders. When I felt the cold metal of his flask against my lips, I drank until the liquid gripped my throat and took my breath. He poured wine and made me drink, and he broke off morsels of meat and fed them to me.

When the warmth and the wine and food had done their work, life seeped back and with it an overwhelming sense of loss. He raised me up then and held me, speaking gentle, comforting words. And now I wept as if the whole of me had been encased in ice which now thawed in the warmth of his arms. And as I put my arms about his neck and drew his face down, seeking more closeness, more comfort, it was as if he took to himself some of my sorrow.

I had planned, oh, how I'd planned—that when he came, if he came, I'd be dressed in the new golden wool, shod in the dainty shoes, clean and combed. Instead I was blown and muddy, swollen-faced and filled with pain.

There must have been many in the village who guessed and thought: The madam, whoring before her husband's laid down! But that night, when he lit the fire for me and waited, they were wrong; for people can put an ugly word to a thing which is wholly good.

FIFTEEN

The next day the village buzzed with talk of the stockingers' troubles. And, in the usual way of gossip, it was said by someone who knew someone who had an aunt living in the Bottoms, that *all* the frames down there had been hacked to pieces and flung into the street. Jack Ketch was to have all the culprits in his noose, and more gibbets were going up on Gallows Hill in readiness.

Stoke Friary was an ant-heap; people running in and out of cottages and across to the Green Man to wring the last drop of fearful excitement from the news, for those who worked the machines were afraid. Most of the frames were rented from a master, but if they were wrecked the stockingers would lose, for how would they live until new frames were brought in and set up? Although they wanted more money for their work, there may have been those who wondered if this was the right way to get it. Wasn't the certain crust better than the possible loaf? The saying 'poor as a stockinger' and memories of bad times in the past were not far from anyone's mind on that day.

The following day, however, we learned that only one frame had been broken, and the Mayor had sworn in special constables and was offering a prize of twenty guineas for the capture of the offenders. Frame-breaking was made a felony, and transportation for seven or more years was the price of it.

Some of this talk I heard from those who called to offer their sympathy. Mrs Hayes from the Old Hall came first, hobbling heavily down the lane. She brought some of her precious stock of used tea-leaves so that I might have a 'second brewing' and some plum cake. I couldn't look at food, but I was grateful for the tea. Alice Brackett came, offering the services of Tommy should I need a man to do jobs for me. Mrs Rowson from the Green Man brought a pile of sewing and told me to 'keep busy'. And Sir John came, threading a bright dream through days which otherwise were heavy and dull. Unable to think of practical matters—the children, Almongate, the future—I found myself turning instead to thoughts of him, as a person turns to prayer in troubled times, to pass the time till evening when he would come to me.

Then at last came a day in early November when, for an hour or two around mid-day, the summer stole back and lay gold across the dying land, and the wall of Almongate cast a long blue shadow to the north. A day when the land outside called and the spread of earth beckoned, and I took up my spade and began to dig.

The soft air washed me gently, a robin watched my spade with interest, someone sang from a boat going downriver, and as the old rhythm took hold of me it eased the knot inside. The smell of freshly turned earth rose, moist, hiding its little secrets; it, like the stars and the wind, would endure. And now that thought, from being a mockery of me and others and our tiny, matterless lives, comforted me. It was promise of an everlasting order. I was alive now, and I could spurn the thoughts I had on the night Matthew died.

The air grew cold and dampness seeped through my clothes. I leaned on the spade to watch the sunset, a streaking stain of crimson and flame, apricot and pale primrose light. This was my land to use as I saw fit, to grub a living from to raise my children, or to leave to the chance sowings of the wind. And it was mine—not by right of freehold, but because I was here, treading it. Mine for this day. That much I could be sure of.

I scraped the earth from my clogs and took the children inside. The lamp burned steadily in the room, and now, with the present securely in its rightful place, I could think of the future. I was at peace.

I came to love my children afresh during the next days. They, like the wind and the stars and the earth, had habits and seasons, and although for a few days I had lost sight of my plans, now my resolve strengthened as I watched them at play, Livvy gripping the rails of the fowl pen and trying to pull herself on to fat little legs, crowing in fair imitation of the birds that jerked themselves agitatedly away from her; Daniel, tied with a long rein to the pear tree, chattering to a robin or absorbed in filling a jar with earth.

The meadowland behind the twitchell lay empty. I had never seen it grazed, but it must belong to someone. Time after time I caught myself thinking about it. If only I could buy a little land, graze some stock, then, after a few years of careful living, buy more land, grow turnips and winter feed so that I could hold the beasts over the winter instead of killing them off and salting the meat. I would grow carrots and fatten more pigs. There'd be a ready market in the town. I'd catch hold of myself then. Land? Stock, turnips? And you—Hester Calladine—a widow with two children and a bare acre that does not belong to you! But if only . . .

I heard myself singing as I put the children to bed, then in this new, happy mood I stripped off my clothes and washed. I shook the lavender grains from my new dress. I hadn't worn it yet, and the wool was soft against the back of my neck. I combed out my hair and put it up, then I opened the book which Miss Olivia had brought me and which still lay, unread, at the back of the cupboard.

I felt a stab of guilt as I began to read. I thought sadly of Matthew for a while: I was doing all the things he had spoken against. And yet, like a butter-

fly emerging into its first warm daylight and stretching creased wings, a sense of freedom grew within
me. I belonged to myself again, and tonight Sir John
would come. Only much later did it occur to me that
no one belonged only to himself, that freedom alone
must be an empty thing with the world a great space
and the butterfly drifting in the wind. Freedom has
its fee: the price of not loving nor being loved, of not
needing nor being needed. Who would seek freedom!

Even in our closest moments I called him 'Sir John',
breathing the words softly against his face, and he
said: 'John, only John,' but to me he was, and always
would be, Sir John. But when I said it I ran the two
words together, 'Sirjohn', and he told me later that the
way I said it made it a love-word.

When I was with him I had a strange feeling sometimes of being able to stand back from my body and
watch myself. And at those times I saw myself grow,
and felt inside myself a layer of shiny, shimmering
droplets, like rain on the spring birches, or dew, or
diamonds—tremble and dance when he touched me. I
even felt sure they must make a tiny music; like the
pendants of a chandelier tapped gently by the
breeze.

'What am I?' I whispered one night as we lay together. 'What is it that makes me aware of every
single part of my body as a separate part? It's as if my
heart grows to fill my skin, and I feel it growing. So
what am I?'

'Sensitive, perhaps?' he said.

'Oh, sense.' I was disappointed. Sense was damping
down the fire when I went out, tying Daniel to the
pear tree to play within my sight, planting more seeds
than I needed in case some should fail. 'Is that all?'
My feeling should have had a beautiful word.

'Not sense,' he said. 'Not sense in the way of ex-
pediency.' He took my hand. 'You have five senses.
Sight: when you look at the sky your sense says: 'Ah,

a cloud, there'll be a storm'. But your sensitivity would see—beauty, possibly, or grandeur.' He folded down my first finger.

'Like seeing you,' I agreed. 'And the other senses?'

'Hearing.' He folded a second finger.

'That's true, too.' His footsteps on the path sent my blood leaping.

'Taste, smell and touch.' He tucked my thumb into my palm. 'There you are, five senses each with two purposes, to select or reject. And this feeling you have is built up from your senses, and so you're sensitive to me. Does that sound self-glorious?'

'Sensitive-to-you,' I said slowly. It was a beautiful word after all. All my senses setting those sparkling drops aquiver.

'Taste, yes—and the smell of you—' I began. 'You smell of fine soap, and linen dried in sunlight and laid in clean closets among spices, I think. I don't know. But I enjoy the smell of you. It enhances—'

He laughed quietly. 'Hester, you never cease to surprise me. Where did you hear that word?'

I felt my face grow hot in the dark as I remembered. 'I don't know. Perhaps something Miss Olivia once said . . . I don't know.' I didn't want to think of that lecherous old relative of hers—uncle, maybe, to the man who lay beside me. 'Touch, yes, I see that, for when you touch me it's—'

'What?' His hand moved.

'I don't know,' I breathed. 'I have no words.'

'Neither you nor anyone else. Poets and bards for centuries have written and sung of it, yet they've never given it full value.'

'But I think they'd go on trying,' I said. 'People will always go on trying, looking for a thing which they know is there.'

'There *was* a poet,' he said, 'who lived a long time ago. He knew when one should stop seeking words and just . . . be.'

'Who was he?'

'His name was Donne.'

Sirjohn raised himself on one elbow and took hold
of my plait of hair which lay over the blanket. He
looped it round his neck, pulling gently so that my
face turned towards him, and his was very close. 'He
wrote—and although he did not have you in mind, my
love—he wrote, "For God's sake hold your tongue and
let me love".'

As we lay quietly watching the moon throw four
squares of light across the bed, I slipped my arm
through his. This I may not do openly, I thought, but
here I may. (Of such small pleasures is love made.)
Here it is my right.

'Happy?' he asked.

'I've never been happier.'

'I don't mean only at this moment. I mean—gener-
ally. Our times together are so brief, such a small
part of our lives. The world has much I could show
you, and yet I cannot. But the rest? Going to the
market, the digging, the back-aches? Trying to do
what you are doing? Are you happy with these?'

'I love Almongate,' I said slowly. 'I love knowing
that I have only to go to the window and look out,
and there beyond the clump of trees, the land rises to
the Old Hall, and you. The market? Well, the walk is
long, and back-ache makes me grateful for a chair,
but—'

'But you haven't answered my question.'

'The things you speak of are my living. I have two
children, and I want them to have a better life than
their father's or mine. I hope that is what they will
want, too. But until they can think for themselves I
must think for them. And even if Daniel wants to
work in a stable as his father did—and there's no
shame in that—I want him to be able to read. Oh, it's
not just the reading, it's knowing that, if he can read,
he can learn about almost anything he wishes. And
perhaps he won't want to know the things a book
could teach him, but he'll have the choice. That is

important. I should like them both to have a comfortable home and not go hungry or cold. And I want a little more for them, too. I can't put a word to it. So, you see, while I can I must live as I do now. How else?'

'I could make you—give you—'

'And have me feel like a paid whore.'

'If you were my *wife* you would have an allowance. And you could never be a whore. Think, Hester, it would make life easier for you. It would assure you of the things you want for your children. And it would give me great pleasure. And it wouldn't be—as you think—in payment.'

'Forgive me for saying that. I didn't mean—'

'I know. But is it so unreasonable for me to want to give? I love you.'

'And I love you. And already your gift to me is something that cannot be measured by money.'

'Love and money. The words fit ill together . . . But why must you tramp the long road to town, stand in the market-place in all weathers? Why should you grub in the soil like some poor cottager—'

'Because I *am* a cottager,' I reminded him. 'And it's thanks to you that I am.'

He made an impatient noise and shifted. 'Can you not understand that in some things I'm rich—rich by your reckoning. Why make life hard for yourself?'

I searched for words. He wanted to do something for me, so, because I loved him, I should let him. Yet by his doing, my life would be changed. *I* would be changed. I should sit idly—could I sit idly? I never had done. Day after day I would tend a few pretty garden flowers, play with my children, sew, wear the yellow wool dress in the afternoons as well as the evenings. He was offering me a life I couldn't live.

I saw myself as on that day in November, staring into the sunset with the smell of the earth rising around me. 'There's the land,' I said, gently, 'and I don't think I could live happily if I didn't work the land.'

'Sometimes the land works *you*,' he said. 'Often, when I was younger, I thought: If only I could leave this place for ever and go back to Italy, to a little town called Padua, to Venice, blue and gold and unlike anywhere else, to Florence, Siena . . . And then I'd remember: Ah, yes, there's the land where the Lindseys have lived for generations. There are the women who deck out their gardens to win my Summer Prize, there's the harvest supper, the Christmas dole . . . There's even that ruined hut by the bridge. So, you see, the land has *me*; *I* have no land.'

'But I have,' I said, 'and because I've never known these places where you speak of, *this* is where I want to be. And although my land is yours—you own it— it's mine because of the work I have given it. I should like to own land. I don't suppose I ever will . . . All my life I've stretched the bit I had to the utmost and then over, until I found myself with just a little more than I could rightfully expect. And, perhaps because of this, my children will . . . It was my mother's way, and it is mine. It *is* me. So I must work here.'

'I know, and I love you for it. It's only because I would like to—'

I bent over and laid my hand against his mouth. 'No,' I said. 'No more talk. "For God's sake hold your tongue . . .".'

Apart from the rhymes of childhood and my grandmother's verses in sing-song rhyme, I hadn't heard poetry before. And that was another of the endless pleasures his loving brought to me.

SIXTEEN

'Love sharpens the senses,' Miss Olivia had said, and Sirjohn had told me what 'senses' were. So, with my senses I explored that perfect winter, and never had life been so vivid and brilliant.

As the short grey days deepened to twilight, then darkness, I waited for him knowing that he, too, was waiting for that moment of meeting. I now understood his need of me. Much of his ordinary living was beyond my understanding; I hadn't shared it and therefore could not realize it completely. But I could see that, after a rich meal, a man might turn with pleasure to a freshly baked crust and a piece of honest cheese; or, whilst at ease in a warm, well-furnished room he might have need of a breath of cold, sharp air. And I believe to him I was those things—the plain fare, the wind that cleanses. To me he was the other things: the rare beauty, the touch of elegance.

We were also bound together by our love of the land, his feeling a deeply-rooted sense of possession and heritage, mine the desire for ownership. But to both of us this feeling was important.

During those evenings when he came to Almongate he took over where Miss Olivia had left off: he brought books and read to me, making me read a page here and there, helping me with the difficult words and explaining their meanings.

There was, too, that other thing of the senses: the sweet urgent clamour of the flesh that says yes and yes and yes, and the quiet time afterwards when the in-

most heart may speak. And as well as this there was
the dream: that one day I'd take his face between my
hands and say: Let us go to those cinnamon-coloured
towns your heart remembers. Let us go together and
be there always. I will work for you. But the dream
was only mine, and I recognized it for what it was.

And so the magic winter opened into green-flecked
spring. My first daffodils jostled the gate-post, the
earliest coltsfoot flowers leaned out on tender, scaly
stems to feel the air. The pear tree put out cramped,
greyish fingers that grew straight in the sunshine until
each green hand held a posy of tiny pale buds.

I was noticing these things, feeling their brilliance in
my soul one morning when everything was wet and
clean from the night's rain. They called me from my
work. The pea-setting must wait. And that, again, was
spring.

As I had some sewing to be returned to Mrs Rowson
this gave me an excuse for doing what I wanted to do.
I walked up the lane thinking how the season was
carefully arranged, down to the newest spear of grass
that pricked the stones. Arranged to cast a yearly spell
over birds and beasts, housewives, bees and young lovers. It was as if God said: 'Look about you, *there* and
there,' and pointed with all the drifting scents that
were spring, before he said: 'Behold my work. Now do
yours.' In the spinney the bluebells were rising out of
their nests of leaves. And although, just now, the flowers clustered closely like violet barleycorns packed
against the stem, soon they would swing, paler and
lazy, beckoning the young men and their girls to walk
among them, to kiss beneath the trees, to lie in the
blue mist. Yes, even the bluebells were part of the
spell.

I turned out of the lane wondering ruefully what
Matthew would have replied to my thoughts. I could
almost see him frown and hear his slow answer: 'Why,
how else could spring be? It's just a season—and a

busy one at that.' And I'd feel like a ragged child caught pretending to be a great lady.

But I could say those things to Sirjohn, and he'd listen without speaking, his head slightly to one side, his mouth tipped kindly. Then he'd cap my thoughts with a bigger thought that took me on a little further, and I'd finish with a better thought than I'd begun with.

More than usually fanciful this morning, I thought that the most important things in my life began with the letter 'l'. Love, learning and land. And there was that other thing, too, luck. I had that. For each day that passed I grew more sure that I was pregnant. I hugged Mrs Rowson's sewing to me as if it could help me contain all the happiness, love, life, everything—my body was too small a vessel to hold so much.

The orange-haired maid at the Green Man let me into the kitchen, then scurried away with a scared glance. I spread out the shifts on the table, and the fire drew out their fresh-air smell.

Mrs Rowson always paid for my sewing with scraps from the kitchen for my pig. I'd often heard Mr Rowson grumble at her for what he called her 'unthrift', and she'd protest that she couldn't abide the stink or sight of the beasts until they lay in slices on her plate with a nice bit of crackling as he well knew, and if he wanted her to keep pigs then he must peg her nose and blindfold her, and how could she get through all her work if he did that? So I got some of the waste stuff.

She came into the kitchen not looking at me. Usually she held up my sewing to examine it and sometimes exclaim over its neatness. But now she did not touch the shifts. She did not speak.

'Have you any more?' I asked. It would save a walk if I took it now.

'No. No more.' Her curt manner puzzled me, her eyes slid everywhere to avoid mine.

'But—the new curtains for the attic—' I began.

'The old ones will do a few more turns. No, that's all. For now,' she added, hastily.

'Oh . . . Then I'll get back. I've left the children . . .'

'Yes.'

No mention of the pig pail. Should I ask for it? But I hesitated; there was something in her tone that hurried me away. Perhaps, after all, she'd decided to raise a few pigs of her own but hadn't liked to say so. But what was there to saying, 'I'm needing all my scraps'? Still, there are folk like that, though they don't usually keep inns and it would account for her manner.

I was almost out of the yard, and into the road when she came running after me. 'A man left a letter for you. Came yesterday.' Again that closed face, and she turned quickly before I'd realized what she'd said and could thank her.

A letter from Miss Olivia, written on thick paper, large and clear so that I might read it more easily. I hurried on, forgetting that I'd meant to call in at Alice Brackett's to tell Tommy to come the next day.

The sun was climbing and the paved causeway shone. A blackbird sat on a post wiping his beak, first one side then the other. He watched me with bright eyes, scolded and flew low across the road. I forgot Mrs Rowson's unfriendly eyes as I hurried down to Almongate. Livvy was still asleep—the thunder during the night had woken her—and Daniel, tied into a chair for safety, crooned to the little wooden donkey Sirjohn had brought him. He pulled the woolly tail, and the donkey lifted his head. Daniel shouted, 'Mamma,' and grinned, and I gave him a hug as I untied the cord and set him on his feet. Then I read my letter.

Miss Olivia wrote that she had had the news of Matthew's death from her father some time ago and had been distressed to hear of the accident. These were troubled times and likely to become harder for some. She was thankful that the winter was over for the east

winds had been excessively cold. She was happy to
tell me that she was to have a child, and what better
season was there for imparting such glad news? Was I
progressing with my writing? Her husband was unwell as he had taken a chill, but she was hopeful that,
with the coming of better weather, he would soon be
restored. She'd welcome a letter from me and was my
friend, Olivia Nicholson. Then, below her name, she'd
written: 'The tone of my father's letter showed him
well content. Are you, too, content, dear Hester?'

I smiled as I folded the paper and laid it away. I was
loth to start on the peas. Well, why should I? My mood
persisted: I'd take a holiday. This morning I would
practise my letters, and this afternoon I'd take the children to the river. Tonight I'd reply to Miss Olivia, I
smiled again at the memory of her sly probing.

With the children asleep in bed, I was sitting down to
answer the letter when I remembered that I still hadn't
seen Alice about Tommy coming to help. We must
make an early start if I were to catch up on my
holiday. I reached her cottage just as she was closing
the door behind her. She stopped with her hand on
the latch.

'Oh . . .' she said, confused. 'I was just coming to see
you.' She backed inside. Her face, pale as elderflowers,
was unhappy.

'Is something wrong?' I asked, slipping the shawl
from my head.

'That's what I was coming to see you about.'

'Is it Tommy?'

'Tommy?' She spoke the name as if she'd never heard
it before. 'No—'

'Who, then? One of the other children?'

'It's . . . you,' she said.

'Oh.' Of course, I'd expected it. It couldn't go unnoticed in Stoke Friary that before I was long widowed
the Squire was calling on me, and I had known that
the busybodies would squeeze all they could from it.

I recalled Mrs Rowson's manner that morning. So *that* was it. And no doubt Alice felt that she must warn me.

'Well,' I said, briskly, 'out with it. I can't see what it has to do with anyone else, but you said you were coming to see me, so let's not waste time.'

She turned. The firelight scooped deep hollows round her eyes. 'They're saying . . . I don't know how to tell you—'

'Alice,' I said, gently, 'just tell me. Never mind how.'

'That—that you use witchcraft.'

I was so astonished that I could only stare at her. Then, after a moment, I began to laugh. 'You ninny,' I gasped. 'Somebody's been taking you for a fool. Me— a witch? Anyway, witches belong to the old days.'

'Don't *laugh*.' Her face worked like dough kneaded from within. 'For pity's sake don't laugh, Hester. It's unlucky.'

'You mean . . . you—believe?'

I reached out to take her hand, but she backed away. 'All right,' I said, hurt by her movement, 'I'll promise not to laugh if you'll tell me why, in heaven's name, I've suddenly become a witch.'

'It's not just—suddenly. It's partly to do with you coming to Stoke Friary and the Squire having that fall in the spinney and Matthew being on hand and getting a job and Almongate all because of it. As if you'd willed it so.'

'But that was more than two years ago. Why haven't I heard this tale before?'

'I don't know,' she said, weakly. 'I never heard it 'til . . . Perhaps it wasn't spoken of before. But now, with you and Sir . . . Folk see things.' She stopped, reddened, and went on: 'It's as if you can make things happen the way you want.'

'I can't. No one can—not when those things concern another person. Have some sense, Alice. I do—well—

my best, I suppose, with what I have. Isn't that what most of us do? You? Tommy?'

'Ah. That's another thing. Tommy. He used to take fits regular. Now he ain't had one since August.'

I stared. 'And you're—*blaming* me for that? Aren't you pleased he's so much better?'

'Course I am. But—well, he works for you, don't he? So it's as if you sort of protected him. They say the devil looks after his own . . .'

'Protected him? Alice, how *could* I? Sometimes things happen in a certain way—no one knows why.'

She didn't answer, and now the accusation which had seemed so foolish was catching me up in its horror. The fire rustled; outside the wind was rising, and the child in the bed by the far wall stirred and whimpered in his sleep. Alice's face was troubled and ashamed, and suddenly I recognized her courage. If people really did think that I was a witch, then she was a brave woman to have me here and tell me so.

'Alice,' I began, softly, 'listen. In the village where I used to live there was an old man. He was afraid of illness—even the slightest cold—and to keep himself clear he wore a little linen bag round his neck. It held a dead mouse and some bits of mashed garlic. He said it frightened off the sickness. Perhaps it did. It also frightened off folk: it stank so badly that no one wanted to be near him. So sometimes he escaped the sickness that was going through the village.'

'But I don't see—'

'Look. I gave Tommy a job. First he made Manna's little cart and I was pleased and said so. I thought of him—not as Tommy Brackett who took fits—but as a good worker, and clever. Perhaps that gave him some kind of strength he never had before. I don't know . . . I just don't know . . . But what I'm trying to say is that often there's more than one reason why a thing is so.'

'That wouldn't have anything to do with his fits.

They come on him, sudden-like, for no reason. And they say that even Master Roland heeds you—that you can make him quiet just by touching him. And he's a zany.'

I sighed. 'Then tell me this: would I have wished Matthew dead?'

'You might,' she said, 'if it made things easier for you and—' She looked at me, closed her eyes for a moment, then hurried on. 'Oh, Hester, I'm sorry. *I* can't help what they're saying, and I don't *want* to believe—'

'But you do.'

'No. No, I don't—know . . . There does seem a kind of sense to it all, the way Annie Fletcher—'

'Ah,' I pounced. 'Annie. I might've known she'd had a hand in it. Well, if any word of mine could make you sure that I'm not a witch you have it. I'm prepared for some folk not to like me, for Annie to be jealous. She thinks I took Almongate from her, and spoiled her chances of marrying Jack Hallam. That's the root of it. But—witchcraft. *Now*, in these times?' Despite my anger I began to laugh again.

'Hush. Don't. I tell you it's unlucky to laugh about it. Witchcraft and ill-wishing ain't so long dead as you might think. My grandfather's uncle that lived over Leicester way remembered a swimming. Whole family of 'em there was, tied together and thrashing out like frogs. And only eleven years ago a woman living alone out by the turnpike set her dog on to a gyppo, and in a few days the dog started frothing and chasing its tail, then it bit her. She died soon after, raving at her window, and none would go near her. And all because she'd cleared a gyppo off her land. He'd spelled her, y'see. So you can't blame folk for thinking . . . It happened once, and witches had children same as other folk. A thing like that could get passed on—like crossed eyes or duck toes.'

'I see.' Suddenly I felt tired. 'Well, thank you for telling me.'

'You won't say owt to Squire, will you? I mean about Annie. She'd most like lose her job.'

'And doubtless starve to death, and that would make me a murderer as well as a witch. No, I won't say anything—except to Annie, and I'll have plenty to say to her when I see her.' Then, remembering Mrs Rowson's face that morning, I said, 'Alice, do—does *everyone* believe this tale?'

'I dunno. But you being a stranger—'

'I've been here two years,' I reminded her.

'Yes, but that's kind of new, isn't it? Most of us have been here all our lives.'

I got up. There seemed no more to be said. 'I really came to see about Tommy giving me a hand tomorrow, but I suppose I must learn to do without him now.'

She sat with her head bent, and I thought she wasn't going to answer. 'I'm sorry you don't believe me, and I'll miss your friendship, Alice.' I went to the door.

'You bought me this,' she murmured.

I turned. She was fingering the blue stuff of her shirt. 'The first new gown I'd had in a donkey's age. I remember you standing in the doorway with the cloth heaped in your arms.'

That had been the day I'd bought my amber wool, and in the shop I'd thought what a help Alice had been, and I'd wanted to give her a present. 'That was a long time ago,' I murmured, and indeed it seemed so. A whole lifetime ago.

'Wait.' She stood up and put her hand on my arm. 'I'm sorry it had to be me who told you, but I thought it only right you should know why folks . . . And about believing the tale—well, I don't know that I do, but I don't know that I don't, either. And I've had troubles enough in my life . . .'

I nodded. 'Yes. Goodnight, then.'

'About Tommy. I been thinking—like you said, he's better than he was, and mebbe he'll want to make up his own mind who he works for. You been good to him, and don't think I'm not grateful.'

Out in the road I drew in great gulps of the night air. I felt sick. Such a stupid, unbelievable story, yet even Alice who knew me well didn't *disbelieve* it. So what of the others? Unlikely though it had seemed at first, how many had listened and nodded and thought? Would they now watch me more closely, searching for a hidden meaning in everything I did? And would they blame me for what went wrong in their own lives? And what would they *do* to me?

I riddled my brains trying to recall all I'd ever heard about witchcraft. In the old days there'd been that awful shaming search for the third nipple. There'd been witch-pricking. And then the flames or the gallows. Oh, but that was long, long ago. A hundred and fifty years . . .

There'd been an old woman, though, in Saxtoft . . . Oh, God, yes, I remembered her now. I'd been small at the time, not more than five years old, but the older children shouted after her, mocking her crooked walk. She'd screamed senseless words at them, and they broke the windows of her cottage. Then, one year after a bad harvest, a sickness had swept the village and many children died. And one morning she got up and found that someone had cut the hind legs off her old dog and had left him to die.

Now, with the warmth of the day gone and the wind tearing the clouds apart so that the moon shone fitfully, the story came back and chilled me, and at the memory of these images my sickness renewed itself.

Then it left me. Suddenly. Like a pail being emptied all at once. I began to run, heavy-footed, stumbling and turning my ankle. Sweat gathered and ran down my ribs. My heart thumped stiflingly in my throat and a voice sobbed in my head: 'Sweet Christ, let them be safe. Let me run faster. Let nothing have happened to them. My children—let them be safe.'

I reached Almongate with my breath tearing my lungs. My hand fumbled for a desperate age on the latch, then I half fell into the kitchen.

SEVENTEEN

Just for a moment I stood inside almost fainting with fright, my hand slack on the latch behind me. Then, as the outstretched legs uncrossed and the body in the high-backed chair leaned forward, I heard my breath go with a sound of ripping linen. Of course. *He* was waiting for me. How could it be otherwise?

Somehow I found my way to the chair opposite him. Already limp, relief weakened me further, and I dropped into the seat, trying to quieten my breathing, bending to ease the cramp in my side, pushing back tumbled hair—all at the same time. And trying to smile.

'Well,' he said gently, 'I confess I'm curious. Is there some kind of troll abroad tonight to hurry you so?'

'I ran,' I whispered, smoothing my hair with shaking hands, 'to you. I hoped you—might—be here.'

He came over and raised me up. His hands were warm, safe. 'How flustered you are, Hester. See—your heart—it's like a frightened bird.'

I looked down, and sure enough the bodice of my gown was pulsing. 'Indeed, I ran very quickly,' I murmured against his shoulder.

His hands comforted me. 'And I never imagined I merited such effort.' He was teasing.

'Oh, but you do, and much, much more.' He held me until I was calmer and could re-shape my thoughts.

'There,' I said, moving away, 'I feel steadier now.'

'Then a glass of wine, I think,' he said, pleasantly.

And, in the same tone: 'What is it, my sweet? You've had a bad fright, I'd say. Be done with this tale of running to *me*. It's more than that.'

'There *is* nothing more than that.' I raised my glass, smiling, flirting foolishly. 'Your health, my sweet sir.' I sipped slowly to gain time. Should I tell him or not? If I said just what had sped my feet, what then? It might bring a laugh at the time of telling—as it had with me at first—but afterwards, what? Would he go back to the Old Hall thinking, considering, then decide that *he* was the cause of it and so would visit me no more? If he were afraid for me, then, out of kindness, no, love—would he not cease the attention which drove a jealous girl to speak out against me? How well did I really know him? On the other hand, he might think I needed him more than ever now. But I couldn't be *sure*.

With the knowledge that my children were safe, and in the reassuring ordinariness of the kitchen, my fear for the moment was stilled, and Annie's story seemed completely crazy. After all, when this little bladder had been kicked round long enough it would collapse, and something else would happen to catch tongue and ear. So the devil with you, Annie Fletcher, I thought, and may he rot your jealous tongue. And there, I thought with satisfaction, you'll have your proof of whether or not I am a witch—but I'll warrant your tongue will still be clacking for a good many tomorrows.

I set down my glass. 'Come,' I said. 'You haven't kissed me yet. And now that I have caught my breath I'm ready to lose it again.'

'There's something—strange about you tonight,' he said.

'It's spring.' I remembered with wonder my feeling of that morning—could it have been only *that* morning? 'Some folks are starstruck, moonstruck. I'm springstruck. Should I be dull and flat after such a day?'

He laughed and caught hold of me then. 'Not you. Not after *any* day.'

Later, still anxious to avoid any questioning about what now seemed unreal, I said: 'I've had the Lindseys well in sight today. I saw Roland and Miss Goodbody this afternoon when I was coming back from the river—' I quickly scored out the memory of Miss Goodbody dragging Roland hurriedly away from me when he would have stopped. So she, too, had heard! 'And,' I rushed on, 'I had a letter from Olivia.' It was the first time I hadn't used the "Miss". 'She wrote that your last letter to her showed you were content. She asked if I was.'

'And are you?'

I smoothed his hair, and said softly: 'As you well know. But—sometimes I think it strange that a daughter should want . . . should give her blessing to . . . *this* —for her father.'

'What do you mean—*this*?'

'Well,' my gesture included the guttering candle, the ash-strewn hearth, the huddle of clothes on the floor. 'Love in a cottage—a woman with earth on her hands and two children in the upstairs room. Someone you could never take to the Assembly Rooms or the races or be seen with at the theatre. You should have perfume and satins, fine manners, music—'

'Those are trimmings—gew-gaws,' he said. 'This is the important part, and it's enough—probably more than I deserve. As for Olivia giving her blessing, as you put it—well, she knows me. Of them all—eight children—I'm left with three.' He stared into the dying fire and I leaned forward and threw on a billet of wood. The sudden flame lit up the sadness in his face. 'Dominic,' he went on, 'emptied before he's twenty-one. He's . . . even as a child he was never other than . . . It was years before I'd admit it. One's own children are special; one makes them so, and I was reluctant to acknowledge that I cannot even like him. God help the people of Stoke Friary when I'm gone. I'm endeavouring to do what I can to safeguard them, but . . . And then, young Roland—his mother calls him the "Bedlamite".'

'But he's not mad,' I protested. 'He's childlike, that's all.'

'To many it's the same thing. He'll never be a man should he live to be ninety. So, you see, out of three children, there's only one *real* person. Olivia. I miss her very much.'

'And I. She wrote—did you know?—that she is to have a child.'

'She hadn't told me.'

'It's only lately that she's known. She will make a good mother. She should have a lot of children,' I said, hugging my own secret to myself.

'It pleases me that she finds marriage so good. They are very much in love. When many marriages are a matter of linking acres with acres or titles to purses, then to have love is to be lucky indeed.' He smiled at me. 'As I very well know.' He tilted my face and kissed me. 'Look, my sweet, I've brought you a present.'

I unfolded the muslin wrapping and shook out a length of French silk, red—so dark as to be almost black—and embroidered with tiny flowers. Never had I touched anything so fine, not even when I was working on Olivia's wardrobe.

'And these to wear with it,' he said, reaching into his pocket and taking out a flat leather box.

'Rubies,' I breathed. 'But they must have cost a great deal of money. I don't think—'

'Don't you like them?'

'How could I not? They're beautiful. But *rubies*. So grand.'

'Not rubies,' he said. 'Garnets, and infinitely cheaper if it makes you feel happier, you little puritan.'

I sat up, naked, only the ear-bobs tapping my cheeks, and I told him about the baby. Afterwards, whenever I wore those ear bobs, I remembered the joy of that evening which had begun so horribly.

After he'd gone I sat until the room grew cold. With his going my fear returned. I sat with my ears stretched for the slightest sound. How many noises there are in a night which one would swear held only sleep. How many tiny sounds when one is listening for—what? How many times—without moving—did I look over my shoulder? At last, cramped and chilled, I went upstairs. I must have slept at last for I dreamed that I was tied to my bed, and Master Roland, wearing the parson's old-fashioned full-bottomed wig, was bending over me saying in the parson's reedy voice: 'Suffer ye not that a witch shall live.' As he spoke the banging started. Manna barked. Livvy cried. They've come for me, I thought, as Daniel called out. I tried to rise from the bed, but I couldn't. My limbs were leaden. Then Master Roland faded, Livvy's crying grew louder, Daniel was tugging at my shift. I must hide the children. The banging went on.

I made an effort that brought sweat pricking out through my skin. I swung my legs to the floor and stood, fighting the nausea that welled up. I shook off Daniel's hand and crept to the window, pressing my back to the wall and peering sideways and down, just as a figure stood back from the door and looked up. Tommy Brackett. I went soft with relief.

'Stay,' I said to Daniel. 'Stay with Livvy for a moment.'

'You wanted me this morning?' Tommy asked when I got to the door.

Still fighting the sickness that made him small and far away, I said faintly: 'There's work if you like.'

He nodded and scraped his feet. 'You all right, Missis?' I murmured something. ''Cos you don't want to 'eed what they're saying—about . . .'

'No.'

'But what you done to them lettuces?'

I stared at him; he wavered and then grew still. With an effort I pushed myself from the door post and, still unshod, I followed him across the cold soil.

There was a sheltered corner in the garden where, if the season was ahead, I nursed along a few plants. I'd learned the sense of selling on an early market, and this year I had a couple of score of lettuces. Now they lay scattered, uprooted, the first white roots pitiful against the dark earth.

Tommy looked at me questioningly. I shook my head.

'Now, who'd want to do a daft thing like that? Look, Missis, you'll catch your death standin' about like that. You're looking a bit dowly. Get back inside and I'll dibble these back in. It's better than nowt.'

I touched his shoulder and turned. I reached the side wall as the nausea flooded up, and I bent over and gave in to it.

Later, I took out my money, and after setting aside a little, I called Tommy in.

'I want a dog,' I said. 'A good, fierce guard dog. Do you know of one? I could pay.'

He squinted for a moment. 'Only Jack Hallam's owd bitch—she's in whelp, and she's a right savager. I could ask him.'

'Yes. And now when I go to market I must take both children—I don't think I can ask your mother to look after Daniel. But I don't want to make Manna's load heavier than I must, so I need a light seat for Dan . . .'

'A sling,' Tommy said, surprising me with his quick thought. 'It could hang between the shafts.'

'Can you do it for me?'

'Course.'

'Thank you, Tommy. You're a great help to me, and I'm grateful.'

He shuffled his feet, pleased. 'I told you not to bother about what folks is saying. Everyone don't think the same way. I don't believe it, and I don't reckon my mother does—not really.'

'Thank you,' I said, and nodded dumbly.

When he'd gone I sat sipping a mug of hot water. Manna came over and laid his head against my knee. 'As for you,' I said, 'You've been eating your head off all winter, but from now on you're going to be carrying a heavier load. Like me.'

EIGHTEEN

In Alice's kitchen I had laughed, then I had been angry. But laughter and anger are ordinary, everyday feelings, soon forgotten. What I felt now was something different; it stayed with me and I had no exact word to put to it.

There was loneliness, yes—of a kind I'd never known. For the first time I saw suspicion in the eyes of people who'd once stopped to gossip, to share a little of their lives with me, to speak to my children. Now, as I walked along the causeway, the women pulling vegetables in their gardens or throwing scraps to their fowls would retreat inside and close their doors. And once I came back from the town to find the word 'wych' painted on the door of Almongate. The limewash had run from the ill-formed letters like tear trails. As I wiped them away I felt thankful that the word hadn't been written in tar, then I was angry with myself for being thankful. Thankful to be wrongly called a witch? But nevertheless I was grateful that the word could be easily washed away. It was the other things that lingered.

A stone was thrown once, but when I looked round I saw no one; so, after a few days, I started to take another path to the town, going along the track by the river to join the road beyond the village where the chances of meeting anyone were less likely. And, for the first time since coming to Stoke Friary, I was not anxious to return at the end of the day.

Part of me still wondered that anyone could believe

this story: witches belonged to an age long past when
people looked for an explanation if things went wrong.
And yet, other old ways stayed with us: touching
wood, the horseshoe over the door, the green bough
at Christmas. Olivia had told me that some of these
had their roots in the ancient days when people wor-
shipped ancient gods, yet I accepted these with no
more thought than I gave to breathing and for no
other reason than that it had always been so. Perhaps
believing in witches was the same. I found myself
thinking about it too often and, in the end, I did not
know what to think.

At times I wished I could talk about it to Sirjohn.
When he said: 'Hester, you look unwell. No market
tomorrow,' or: 'Tonight you will rest and I shall read
to you,' I wanted to tell him the reason, but I could
not lest it smirched me in his eyes. So even my pleasure
of him was touched by this thing, and when I saw my
face in the mirror growing pinched and hunted-look-
ing I thought, sadly, soon he will not want me any
more.

Then would be the time to go, to leave Stoke Friary
with my children. Annie, then, might have Almongate.
She would have got her way. Would that make *her* a
witch?

During those weeks Tommy was a great help to me.
It was as if, suddenly, he'd taken a great stride into
manhood and was no longer the rather slow boy to
whom I must say: 'Tomorrow we will do this,' or
'Tommy, perhaps it would be better done in this way.'
Now, he told *me*. Often he'd take the tool from my
hand and say: 'You go and set you down for a bit.
I'll finish this.' I was glad to let him take charge; my
old spirit had gone.

One day I said: 'If we go on like this I'll be working
for you.'

And he said: 'Oh, no, Missis. When all's said and
done this is your place, and I'm glad I've got this
job.'

I turned away so that he could not see my tears.

So, apart from Sirjohn and the women I met at the market, I rarely spoke to anyone until the day Jack Hallam came.

His bitch had whelped, and when the pups were ready to leave their mother Tommy brought Jack to see me. His hands, rawboned and rough, made the pup cradled within them seem small.

It was the first time I'd seen him since the night of Matthew's death, and he was gaunter and shabbier. But he still had that level straight look as if his thinness and patches were a part of him that needed neither explanation nor excuse. As I watched him come up the path I could see why Annie wanted him.

He ducked inside the doorway and stood looking round. He must have noticed the few comforts that had appeared since the last time he'd stood there, but he said nothing. And if he'd heard the tale of my witchcraft—as surely he must—there was no suspicion in his eyes, no sly smile to show it. Perhaps he had his own ideas about women's gossip.

'Tommy said you wanted a good dog,' he began, 'and I reckon this little 'un'll do you. I don't know who fathered him, but he must have been a brave 'un to take on my Nell—she's not like most bitches in season. He's a bit on the short side, but he'll feed up. And there's nowt like red meat to keep him sharp,' he added, laughing.

'He might get it sometimes,' I said, taking the pup and wincing as its needle-sharp teeth found my thumb.

'Then he'll be luckier than most. Folks're meat-hungry—let alone dogs.'

'How much are you asking?' I said.

'Naw—glad to get a home for him. Besides, I always felt bad about—about what happened that night—the way I let you walk into town by yourself.'

'I *wanted* to go alone,' I reminded him. 'There's no call for you to feel bad about—anything. I remember that you *did* offer to go with me. Now, how much? I told Tommy I'd pay for a good watch dog, and pay I will.'

'And I'll not take a penny. Like I said, I'm pleased he's going to a good home where he'll get,' his eyes twinkled, 'his red meat.' Then: 'Hear, that, Little Un?' he said to the pup.

'I've got an arrangement with the man in the Shambles for scraps . . . I began. Then: 'You're proud, and a new pair of boots wouldn't come amiss.'

He looked down at his feet and grinned. 'I manage,' he said.

I looked at Tommy. He shrugged. So he wasn't going to be of any help in the matter of payment.

'There'll be a pig to be killed in October,' I said. 'You could help then. There'd be something for you.'

'Ah, well, if it's work you're giving away, that'd be different. And I can't remember the last time I set my teeth into a dish of chitterlings. Work's scarce, and folks've got long memories for my words.'

'And what were your words?'

'Why, nowt so unreasonable; only that to work well you need a full belly—and a bit more.' He went over to the window. 'You've made a nice little place out of this piece here.'

'Tommy and I,' I said. 'We've both worked at it.'

'I can see that. Well, I'd best be going. Squire's sprinkling his drive again, I hear, and there may be a few hours for me at the gravel hole. See you on pig-killing day, then.'

'You won't see *me*,' I said.

'No, she'd run a mile from a killing,' Tommy said, dotingly.

Jack shook his head at my silliness and went off up the path, straight and tough as a leather thong.

Annie didn't deserve him.

On the first Monday in October when Jack Hallam arrived, I was ready for the town. The day was clear with a thin tooth of frost, and I was anxious to be away before the knives were sharpened and the big board set across the trestles. One day, perhaps, I'd get over the sickness that a pig-killing brought; after all, I'd reared the beast for the table. But still the old pity was there for an animal I'd fed and housed and even talked to during its life, and I wanted to see no part of the preparation to end it. I resolutely turned my eyes away from the big tub that Tommy was dragging out, and after a few last-minute instructions I stepped out briskly into the fine morning.

I had never been to any of the town dressmakers before, but I reckoned that my money was as good as anyone's and, besides, I didn't fancy sewing the beautiful dark red silk myself in case I spoiled it. I intended to have it made up into a gown that would be loose and comfortable just now, but that could be altered when I was back to my right shape again. I'd already chosen the dressmaker's—a trim little place, well-painted and neat, down a quiet side street running from the market-place.

I opened the blue door and stood for a moment looking round. The panelled walls were painted a pale apple-green, and on some of the panels hung sketches of elegant ladies in fashionable gowns. Just inside the door stood a tiny inlaid table with a brass bell on it. I lifted it; it tinkled. A gentleman sitting on one of the gilt chairs opposite the door shook out his paper and looked up. I recognized him immediately. Mr Dominic. He must be waiting for his wife. He stared at me for a moment with his yellowish eyes, then looked back to his paper as a middle-aged woman, very elaborately dressed, came through a green silk curtain. Her smile wavered a little as she saw me, and my amber wool dress felt shoddy and ill-made, and far, far too tight. But she came on, her smile widening and setting. It didn't touch her eyes; they remained sharp and hard as wet flints.

'If you will come with me I'll send someone to you

with some samples,' she said. 'You may make a selection at your leisure. What is your preference? Wool, perhaps? Or something a little more delicate? I have some very fine—'

'I have my own—silk . . .'

The smile was still there, but she spoke as if to a half-witted child. 'I'm afraid,' she began, loftily. 'That it is not usual for—'

'Then in that case I'll find somewhere where it is—' I turned, aware that Dominic had lowered his paper and was following our conversation with interest. A hot, red blush crept up my neck.

A thin hand stayed me. 'I *did* say *usual* did I not?' the woman chided, playfully. 'And just at the moment I am not holding a large quantity of materials. With fashion so capricious . . . This may not be London, but that is no reason why we should look like farmers' wives—do you not agree?' Again those hard eyes swept my dress. 'Now, if I may see—'

I shook out the silk and surprised a look of admiration on her face. 'Ye—es, quite splendid . . .' She lifted the curtain and motioned me to go through. 'I'll take your measure, then we can discuss styles. And, oh, the styles this season—never, I declare, has there been anything quite so—'

As I passed into the small corridor I felt Dominic's eyes on my back, and I knew with certainty that Madam's tape would measure me no more closely than did they.

The following week Sirjohn went to Hull to attend to some urgent business, after which he was to stay with Olivia for a few days. During his absence Dominic—whose wife was visiting her mother in London—was to stay at the Old Hall to keep Lady Lindsey company. October was a popular month for visits for soon the roads would be bad, and added to the hazards of highwaymen and footpads was that of vast holes—almost small ponds—which had been known to swallow up both horse and rider. The days were fast closing in now, and on the Wednesday it seemed that winter was already come.

After I had put the children to bed I took up my sewing and settled down for the evening. Presently my fingers tired, so I turned down the lamp and gave myself up for a hour to that delightful half-waking, half-dozing idleness when the mind moves gently. And mine, as usual, moved towards Sirjohn. I missed his visits; I missed the thought that tonight he might come. Fond as I was of Tommy, I longed for some *real* company, talk of things other than the garden. And despite my pregnancy—or perhaps because of it—I felt ripe and wanton and needful of him, so when I heard the first hoof-falls my mind shouted 'You're home early,' and I hurriedly smoothed my hair, threw more wood on to the fire, set out wine and two glasses. When Little Un growled from his shelter by the gate I opened the door and went out into the damp night.

But the hand that closed over mine was strange, and I backed away, catching my breath with sudden fear. This, then, was what I had been dreading. At last, *this* was where all the talk led. Of course, I thought, dully, they'd wait until Sirjohn was safely out of the way before they'd do anything. Then, as the light from the cottage caught the face of the man who still gripped my hand, I saw that it was Dominic.

The sudden rush of relief ebbed quickly as he bent forward and peered into my face. 'Well,' he drawled, 'I expected some kind of welcome, certainly, but not such a flattering reception. Why, I've seen you some-where . . . Now, where— Well, damned if it ain't the sleek little sparrow whose silk made that old bitch's eyes pop. And to think you're my father's doxy, and by the looks of it—' his eyes raked my body '—he hasn't been wasting his time. What are you hoping to breed? Another slight-witted pretty boy like Roland?' He laughed, a high, snickering noise that set my teeth on edge.

'Well? Now that I'm here aren't you going to remember your manners? The wine—the glasses,' he prompted. Then, as I made no move, he filled the glasses and handed me one. He shrugged as I made no move to take it and carried it over to the fire, flicked up his coat skirts and sat down in Sirjohn's chair. 'You acquitted yourself well that morning—quite made that little dressmaker look small.'

Still I stood there, unable to speak.

'Deuced funny. I couldn't believe it when I heard that my father—my *worthy*, puritan father of all unlikely persons—was ... Then, thought I, I'll take a look at the little nest he's feathered and at the hen bird there. And sitting, too, by God. And so I find you. Well come, my dear, haven't you anything to say?'

What was it Nancy had told me? 'He fair gives me the horrors.' And yet, and yet, he *was* like his father— like a blurred, stained watercolour of Sirjohn. I should have loved him perhaps, if only for that.

'I am—as you say—your father's doxy. And now that you've seen me perhaps you'd leave. I have nothing to say to you. And I was about to go to bed ...'

'Splendid.' He slewed round in his chair. 'Possibly you would prefer company? Tell me, is not your bed lonely and cold while he's away?'

I didn't answer.

'Not very talkative, are we? I'll warrant you have more to say for yourself when my father's here. Or is it that you have no need for words? Tell me, is he so bedworthy that you *don't* talk? I've known it to be that way, though personally—' he kicked the log and sent a shower of sparks up the chimney '—I would never have judged him to be that much of a man.'

'Please go,' I said, my voice little more than a whisper.

'All in good time, and only when I'm ready. You fascinate me—first so uppity with the dressmaker, now so prim-mouthed. Not that talk is necessary—as you so obviously realize—though often it does entertain. And really you do look rather handsome standing there with the light on one side of your face and the other in shadow. You're unfashionable, of course, and would be too thin without that belly, but you know what they say: the sweetest meat lies near the bone . . .' He laughed again and stood up. 'Come now. Enough of this shyness. You're no green girl. You showed more spirit when I saw you before. And I like a little fire. Oh yes. I've come to see you, my dear; after all, it isn't rare for a son to sup from his father's dish, now is it?'

I backed away, but before I could reach the door his hand shot out and trapped my wrist. He drew me towards him, sickening me with his wine-soured breath. I struggled for a moment, but his hand tightened.

Behind me Manna moved. A sharp nip in the leg, Manna, I prayed. Just enough to make him slacken his hold. But his boots lashed out and I heard it crack on bone. Manna yelped and circled. I struggled again, seeing our shadows, large and grotesque, writhe on the opposite wall. Manna moved forward.

'Call off the dog. Do it, I say, or you'll suffer.'

Faintly, I obeyed and struggled again but weakly, gradually sagging, growing limp, so limp that he could, perhaps, have taken me in that moment. If that was what he wanted. Part of the horror was that I did not know exactly what he wanted of me. Maybe I could have fobbed him off by playing up to him a little, by flirting, half-promising words and glances that would have satisfied him for this night at least. But I couldn't risk it.

He was kissing me, horribly, wetly. Summoning all my strength I pulled away, at the same moment lifting my knee, and I felt it punch into the soft, pendulous belly. He gasped and for an instant let go of me. I was free, reaching for the chimney and for the little log

fork that hung there. I wrenched it from its nail and
turned to face him. Still gasping, and slightly bent to
clutch his belly, he moved back. There was no time
to think. Just now I was the master. I took a step
forward, and again he drew back, but he was recover-
ing himself.

'So that's to be the way of it,' he said, smiling
twistedly. 'You're mad, brandishing that little toy.'

'You're wrong.' I marvelled at my apparent calm-
ness. 'This is a sturdy tool, and I shall use it if I must,
and with all my strength. Nor am I mad, and for that
reason I don't favour the thought of lugging you,
bleeding, out of the house and heaving you across your
saddle.' I jabbed the air to lend my words force.

'Somehow I don't think you will have to. Touch me
with that damned fork and you'll be sorry.'

I fought against the weakness in my legs and pulled
myself up tall. Like that I was almost a head higher
than he. But I badly needed to sit down.

'For the last time,' he grated, watching my arm
warily, 'you bloody little witch, drop that fork, or I'll
have you, by God, and it won't be me who bears the
mark of it.'

'So you've heard,' I said, clutching at the word. And
I laughed. I'll never know how.

'Heard what?' he growled.

'Why, that I'm a witch, of course—as they're saying
in the village. But I didn't know that my fame had
spread to the Old Hall.'

The mask of his face shifted and grinned. He looked
like an animal, a foxy, cruel animal that can wait for
its prey to spend itself and give up. I stepped forward again, but this time he didn't move.

'So we're going to play games, are we? All right. I'll
play. Now, that's a strange bait to try and catch me
with, but all right . . . prove it. I've never bedded a
witch before—it promises to be exciting. I wonder—are
witches made like other women? But let's leave that

for now. You can show me some other time. Just for now prove your words. How will you do it?' He began to snigger. 'Strike me dumb? Wither my limbs? Or perhaps my ears will drop off?'

'You make a mistake,' I told him. 'You think that witches scatter their gift like chaff.' I shook my head. 'They don't. They value their talent and hoard it, using it only when necessary. A little here, a little there, wherever it will do most good—or harm.'

He was laughing now and close enough for me to see the wine stain on his embroidered, cockfighting waistcoat. I knew that I could not keep this up; I was desperate and shaking and afraid. But I must keep playing for time, hoping for—what? Anything that would put an end to this nightmare.

I waved the fork again. 'You tell me to prove it. Do you really think I wait upon your order? How do you know that I haven't already used a little of my talent?'

'Now I know you're mad,' he said, easily. 'Though I do admit that you have talent of a sort—you're bewitching me with this nonsense. Come, show me your power. Brew up your potions. I haven't spent such an entertaining evening for months, nor one which offered so unique a prize at the end.'

He reached for me.

'Tell me,' I said, through stiff lips, 'do you have the language of the gutter on your tongue when you lie with a woman? As your great-uncle did?'

'Now how would you know that?' he said, slowly. 'Ah, yes, my father—'

'I know many things,' I said, 'and it wasn't your father—'

'No, of course not. It wouldn't be. He's too God-worrying to tell you of that old rip, Nicholas. He wouldn't even like to think about him.'

'Witches *do* know things,' I said, taking advantage of the pause. 'People aren't afraid of witches purely for what they do—more for what they might know about folk. It's part of their power.' I stabbed the air with the fork, and the long straight prong scratched his sleeve. He jumped back, his face uncertain.

'Now,' I snapped, 'shall we go on like this until you reach the window. It's behind you. About three paces. And if I must use this—' another jab '—and you don't want to be spitted like a dead fowl, you'll have to go through the window. Either way, you won't be a pretty sight.'

He ducked sideways and stood by the door, his face twisting with rage. 'Damn you, you whore. I'll go as I came. By the door. But I'll be back. Don't doubt it. By Christ I'll be back.' He wrenched open the door, and the flames leapt in the sudden draught so that I could see his terrible face, red and devilish in the glow. 'I intend to know just what kind of pleasures my father buys, and by God I'll take such a sample that you won't be able to lie with him for a month. Don't doubt it. This isn't the end.'

After he'd gone I pushed the bolt home with shaking fingers. The log fork clattered to the floor, and I sank into the chair. I sat for a long time, fighting down the urge to laugh. It was so funny—oh, God, yes, it was funny! To think that Annie's story should have served me so well! To think that I had the wit to use it for my own purpose . . . Oh, yes, it was the funniest thing . . . I heard a strange noise and realized that I *was* laughing and crying and shaking so much that the lop-legged chair chattered against the floor. I bit my tongue hard to still myself as Manna crept from his corner and lay beside me, whimpering and licking his flank. After a while I dragged myself over to the cupboard and splashed out a good measure of the brandy Sirjohn had brought. 'Take a drink if you're low,' he'd said. 'It'll hearten you.'

I tossed it down, shuddering. Was there to be no end to it, I wondered. First a witch and then a whore. And really I was an ordinary woman—the only extraordinary thing in my life was the love Sirjohn had for me. Come home soon, I begged him silently. I cannot bear any more.

NINETEEN

I now had two fears: the one of Dominic returning as he had promised, and the other—that shadowy, shapeless feeling that had stayed with me since the last time I saw Alice, though no one had actually done anything since that one week when the lettuces were uprooted, the stone thrown and the word 'wych' painted on the door. Sometimes I wanted to ask Tommy if they still talked of me in the village, but I was afraid of his answer. So, whenever possible, I took the river track out of the village and saw no one. I was still afraid, but I had grown used to living with my fear and, provided there was no new evidence of everyone's hand against me, I could think of other things.

I had taken Little Un when my fear was at its greatest, when I saw my future as friendless, my safety threatened, thinking that when the dog grew he would be my guard. But now I had to safeguard him, knowing of Dominic's way with animals, so each evening I brought him into the house, dragged the table over to the door, and extravagantly lit several dips, feeling that their brightness made Dominic's threat less menacing.

A few days after his visit we set off for the market. There had been a keen frost, and the pools by the river shone with a web of ice. Manna kept up a steady pace until we came into the town and reached the top of the hill that led down to the market-place. There, to ease the weight of the cart, I always took Livvy from the top tray and sat her astride my hip and set Daniel on his feet to walk beside me, clinging to my skirt.

I was about to help him out of the canvas sling when a man rode out of a side turning and drew level with us. Manna moved forward, and then I saw that a piece of meat had been thrown down and was being drawn along the road, apparently attached to the man's saddle by a cord. Manna lunged, his jaws snapping; Daniel screamed at the sudden movement and tried to struggle out of the sling. I hauled back with all my strength, but the dog's torment and the slope of the road were too great. The cart bounced away from me, rocking crazily. I ran behind, shouting for help. The rider turned suddenly, disappearing into a narrow street and Manna, changing his direction quickly, turned after him. The cart struck a mounting block and overturned. Not Daniel, I thought. Oh, no, not Daniel, too, struck by a mounting block—perhaps the one where Matthew had fallen . . .

When I reached him he was crying and bruised but otherwise unhurt. Weak with relief I untied Manna and righted the cart, seated the children on it and pushed it shakily over the cobbles of the market-place. Why? I kept asking myself. And who? I hadn't seen the horseman's face but I knew the answer. I was a witch so I must be harried and persecuted until, beaten, I left. But before I went I would see Annie. I would tell her where her hatred had led. I would show her the swelling on Daniel's face, the grazed knuckles. I would say—

I looked up suddenly. Dominic was sauntering towards me. He wore the same foxy grin, but this time his eyes showed real amusement. He picked up an egg, held it between his thumb and forefinger, then let it drop on to the stones. 'I trust that you had a pleasant journey?' he said, softly. Then he went. I stared after him.

Quickly I harnessed Manna, took Daniel's hand and lifted Livvy. The children would not ride out of town, although my sense told me that Dominic would not try the same trick twice. Next time it would be something different.

That evening Sirjohn came back. He expressed surprise that I should have to heave the table out of the way before I could open the door to him, and I accounted for my vagary by my pregnancy which was now into the seventh month. The warmth of his greeting and the knowledge that he was back made the bad things easier to bear. Our hours together were so short and so precious that I had no wish to spoil them by mentioning my misfortune. And when he told me that Dominic and his wife, together with Lady Lindsey, were going to London to visit her sister and I knew that I would be free from Dominic's attentions for the next two weeks, at least, my fears were lulled. So our evenings settled back into their comfortable pattern; the sweetness was back in my life. And although our lovemaking was now little more than tenderness on his part and a wish to please on mine, the evenings we spent together still held the old magic which had begun on the night of the Ball.

December opened with a spell of mild, soft weather, drawing out the trumpets of the jasmine, stirring up false hopes that the sad, moping months of January and February could never be. But that, I knew, was only wishfulness, and sure enough, after the middle of the month the weather grew cold again until, on the afternoon of the twenty-third, the sky was thick and heavy, the land lay waiting, and there was the smell of snow in the air.

Lady Lindsey and Dominic had decided that they would keep Christmas in London, and I cherished a hope that Sirjohn would spend Christmas Day with me at Almongate. There was much to do. I had set the bread dough to rise on the hearth; the Christmas Eve market would be busy, and I couldn't hope to get back early: many people, waiting for prices to fall, hung back until the market was closing before buying their

Christmas dinner. So, knowing that I'd get little done in Almongate the following day, I was—in my mother's words—'stocking up jobs beforehand'.

Outside Tommy was plucking and trussing the birds for me to take to market—that way I could carry more. With a wicker skip for the feathers wedged between his knees and a pail for the entrails by his side he sat at a trestle, and from time to time I heard the thud of the cleaver as he took off the heads. From the window I could see him, the tip of his nose red above his grey muffler, his hands purple as they moved among the feathers. I poured him a drink of blackcurrant cordial to warm him, and I was just setting down the kettle when he shouted. I glanced through the window, then I moved as quickly as my bulk would allow, taken by an icy fear that I would not, *could* not reach him in time. Inside the run, he crouched among the spilled feathers by the overturned skip. Roland stood near. And he held the cleaver. As I watched Miss Goodbody darted forward, only to jump back as Roland swung in her direction.

'Roland,' she said, shakily, 'put that down. Do as I bid, you naughty, disobedient boy.'

He seemed not to hear. He was looking at the limp fowls whose necks had so recently been pulled and which were now waiting to join the pale carcases stacked near the cart.

'Go inside,' I called to Miss Goodbody, 'and give an eye to my children. I'll try and find someone to—' and with that I was out into the lane, running awkwardly but as if my life depended upon it.

At the top of the lane I hesitated. Which way? To Bromleys, or to the village? And then I saw Sirjohn riding leisurely round the curve. I started to run again, and when he saw me he spurred on the horse until he was within hearing. 'Roland,' I gasped. 'At—Almongate—he's—the cleaver—'

Already he was past me, stretching the horse to a gallop.

When I got back he was with Roland. Tommy stood at a small distance, and Miss Goodbody had come out of the house, followed by Daniel who stood staring, his thumb halted halfway to his mouth.

'Roland,' Sirjohn was saying, 'I want you to give that to me.'

Roland turned, uncertainly, and Tommy, seizing his chance, scrambled out of the litter of feathers and up the pile of logs stacked against the sty and swung himself on to the low roof.

I made a step forward, but Sirjohn saw me and called: 'It's all right, Hester. Stay there. All of you stay still.' Roland hacked savagely at the air, his beautiful, empty face was twisted with rage, and he was sobbing. Only then did I remember his fondness for chickens. I shut my eyes for a moment; that Miss Goodbody should have chosen this day of all days to walk down the lane!

I opened them to see Tommy brace himself. 'Don't,' I shouted sharply. 'Don't jump. Someone'll get hurt.'

'Hester, go inside,' Sirjohn snapped. 'And stay up there, Tommy. Just be quiet—all of you . . . Now,' he said, gently, 'come here, Roland, and give that to me. You don't want it. To me . . . to—me. Then we'll go home. You shall ride Brandy if you wish, and I'll lead him.' Roland stood like an animal at bay trapped by the closing hounds. Sirjohn moved toward him, his leg gently nudging away the trestle between them. He smiled. 'Just pass it to me, my son, and we'll go.' His voice was very pleasant and soft. 'There'll be a good warm fire, and you shall take your milk and ginger-bread with—'

Gingerbread—of course. Why hadn't I thought of it? I ran inside, took down the jar and fumbled off the lid, tipping out the spicy, sweet-smelling heap on the table. I snatched up a handful and hurried out, wanting to shout but afraid of startling the boy.

A log from the top of the pile, loosened by Tommy's scrambling ascent, broke away and was rolling down, and Roland turned uncertainly. In that moment Sirjohn reached out. Roland swung back quickly, the cleaver held steady in both hands. It struck the snuff-coloured coat. I ran forward shouting: 'No, no, you must not—' but by the time I reached them Sirjohn was doubled over, and already Roland was raising the cleaver.

'No,' I whispered. 'See. These are for you.' He stared at me, then down at the cleaver, then he bent and placed it carefully on the ground between us and held out his hand. I gave him the gingerbread and he offered his cheek. Even at this moment it seemed that the little ceremony that had begun so long ago in the kitchen of the Old Hall must be followed. Quickly I brushed his forehead with my lips. Then I put both arms round Sirjohn, supporting him.

'Tommy!' I looked up to where he still towered against the darkening sky like some sturdy scarecrow uselessly set on the pig-sty roof. 'Tommy, help me, for God's sake. We must get him into the house. You, too, Miss Goodbody.' But she paid no heed; she clung to the doorpost, half-swooning. Roland, his woollen cap a red bud in the greyness, licked his fingers and watched us with interest.

Tommy pushed him out of the way. 'You great sawney,' he shouted. 'What you want to go and do a daft thing like that for?'

I shook my head. 'Leave him, Tommy . . . He doesn't understand . . . Just *help* me.'

Between us we got Sirjohn into the house and on to the bed which Tommy had dragged down. Miss Goodbody and Roland and Daniel followed us in, and Roland went over to Manna who dozed by the fire. Miss Goodbody leaned against the wall, her eyes closed, her face the colour of almonds.

'Tommy, you'll have to ride for the doctor.' I offered up a silent prayer of thanks that Sirjohn had been riding Brandy and not the spirited Saladin. 'But first, bring me the chicken entrails. Go on. Just do as I ask.'

I was thinking furiously and almost crying with the effort of it.

When he came back I took the pail, then scarcely aware of what I was handling I began to smear the chicken ooze over the soles of Sirjohn's fine, polished boots. 'You must tell the doctor that there has been an accident. That Sirjohn slipped and cut himself badly. Nothing more. Do you hear? You, too, Miss Goodbody. This is the way it must *seem* to have happened, otherwise Roland . . . Do you understand? It's important. Now go quickly, Tommy. And tell the doctor to hurry.'

I turned to Sirjohn and gently lifted away the stained clothing, staunching the deep gash from which the blood welled continuously. He opened his eyes, and I fancied that he smiled at me.

Dearest, the doctor is coming. And I'll care for you. Nurse you. I will not let you die. God, let not the strength of my love make my fingers other than gentle . . . Perhaps I spoke the words, perhaps not.

When the doctor had gone Miss Goodbody still sat by the fire, apparently unable to rouse herself. 'You'll have to go,' I said at last. Sirjohn was sleeping now. I splashed some brandy into a mug. 'Drink that. It'll help.'

'Oh, no.' She shuddered away from me. 'It's no drink for a—I've never taken spirits . . .'

'Drink it,' I said, roughly. 'Every drop. Then you must take Roland away. You can't stay here all night. He's all right now—it was just the fowls . . . I'll give you a lantern.'

'He was here before,' she faltered.

'Who? The doctor?' I stared at her.

'No. Roland. One day in spring. We were walking, and I felt unwell. I had to rest against your wall and put my head down. Roland—he came into your garden and pulled out some plants. I couldn't stop him—'

'No. Never mind that now.' I settled her bonnet and put Roland's hand in hers hardly aware of what I was doing, thinking: Yes, of course—the lettuces. I had found them on that dreadful morning after Alice had told me I was a witch. I had seen Roland and Miss Goodbody in the afternoon, and they'd hurried away from me, I thought it was because she, too, had heard the story. It was Roland all the time . . . But that was irrelevant now. I thrust the lantern at her, eager to be alone with Sirjohn, anxious to put all my love into caring for him.

And so the story reached the village, and people said: 'Wasn't it a pity? Just because a lad—a zany at that—hadn't been able to resist playing about with feathers and had picked up a chopper and ran amuck . . . And when his father, afraid that he might do himself a mischief—him being a loony and all—had tried to take it from him, was in the very act of doing so, had it in his hand, in fact, he'd slipped and fallen on the blade.'

And some said: That it had all happened at Almongate wasn't to be wondered at, really. Hadn't Hester Calladine had things her own way for too long; wasn't she getting above herself? It was high time she took a tumble. Justice, that's what it was.

TWENTY

The doctor had ordered complete rest for Sirjohn. He must lie still as his ribs were injured, and should there be any sign of a fever I must send for him. Meanwhile I should keep the wound covered, and no doubt within a day or two suitable arrangements could be made for Sirjohn to be moved to the Old Hall. Quietly I decided that I would make my own arrangements; with Lady Lindsey away there was little point in his going back there to be cared for by servants, and I saw no reason why he should not stay with me until he wanted to go.

The following day he lay still, taking a little broth from time to time and sleeping a lot, and by the next morning he looked much better.

'What day is it?' he asked, reaching out for my hand.

'Christmas Day. And I have a gift for you.'

I brought out the gloves which I had made for him, using as a pattern one of his own which I'd hidden some weeks ago and which he'd thought was lost. Now I was able to return it. He laughed at my deviousness, wincing a little with the pain in his side. 'And I have a gift for you,' he said, 'and what a pity that I haven't brought it with me.'

'No matter. *You* are with me.'

'But, on the other hand, my gift to you *is* here.'

'Oh? I don't see—'

'Let me speak. Do you remember telling me that you would like to own some land?'

I nodded.

'Now you do: ninety acres and this cottage. It was not entailed. I was coming back after seeing Mr Gosling, my lawyer, when I rode down the lane—was it yesterday? No, the day before. All the papers are with him, but the land and cottage are yours. And there is some money, of course—enough to start your farm.' He paused, watching my face, then he said, gently: 'Did you hear me, darling?'

'Yes. But I—can't believe . . .' I shook my head. 'I can't believe any of it. Are you really here now? And have you just given to me Almongate and ninety . . . ? Oh, it's too much . . . too much—'

'Hester—you shouldn't cry—'

'I should. I must. I don't know what else . . . I can't think. Oh, I'm so happy, happy. You can't know . . .' I buried my face in my hands, rocking backwards and forwards. 'I don't know what to say. You're so good to me. It makes me afraid.'

'Why afraid?' He moved my hands away and with his fingers gently dried my tears.

'Because, oh, because it doesn't seem possible that anyone could be given so much without having to pay for it,' I said, slowly.

'Silly girl. It's little enough, and I always wanted to take care of you, but you wouldn't let me. I watched you struggle when everything was against you. You were so proud, so grateful for so very little. It is my greatest pleasure to give to you.'

I bent forward and kissed him. 'I do love you, you know,' I whispered, and began to weep again.

'I think that you should take a drop of brandy to steady yourself. And after that I should like you to read to me because I am very sick.' He lay back with his eyes closed.

I laughed a little then, as he had intended me to do, and he drew my face down and brushed my wet eyes with his mouth. Then he kissed my lips, and it wasn't the kiss of a very sick man.

* * *

Perhaps it was wrong of me to enjoy those days: I
knew that he was weak and that the pain in his side
troubled him. I knew, too, that for a man who loved
the outside world his confinement could only be irk-
some. But, even so, I gloried in his dependence upon
me. His eyes followed my every movement, and I had
only to take four steps and reach out my hand and I
could touch him—not for just an hour or two, but for
every hour of the day and night. It was pure joy to be
his gaoler and his nurse, to feed him, wash him, to
watch his face while he slept.

Another thing, too, had made me happy. The day
after the accident—as I now thought of it—Alice Brackett had come to Almongate.

'I thought perhaps you'd like me to take the children,' she began, 'you bein' so busy and all.' She craned
her neck to stare at Sirjohn, and when she saw that he
was watching her she reddened and sketched a little
bob. I drew her outside and spoke in a low voice.

'It's kind of you, but . . . I'm supposed to be a witch,
remember?'

For a moment she couldn't meet my eyes. Then she
said, 'I'm sorry, Hester. I feel so ashamed—me telling
you about it that night and sorta half believing it myself. But now . . .'

'Yes?' I waited.

'Well, the story's been put straight. Oh, it *did* go
round the village last spring, and some believed it
and some didn't. Then, when Squire had this accident
Annie brought up the story again. And this time Mrs
Hayes got to hear about it. She hadn't heard the tale
before . . . Funny, that, her working with Annie and
all—but that's how it was. Anyway, she had a lot to
say about you bein' her best worker and that if you
was a witch she'd be happy to fill her kitchen with
witches instead of the slovens she's got. She made it all
sound so *ordinary*, like. One of the maids at the Hall
told me. She raged on and on at Annie, told her that
she was just plain jealous, but that was no reason to

make up tales. Then she said Annie would have to go, that the Old Hall had always been a good place for servants, but that Annie spoiled it with her trouble-making and she didn't deserve to work there any longer. Then the housekeeper, Mrs—'

'Broome,' I said.

'Yes. Well, she said it was all a silly tale that no right-thinking God-fearing person would have believed anyway, but she said if it would restore peace in the kitchen Annie must go and put the story straight. And Mrs Hayes said, "Aye, and I'll see that she does."'

I stood quietly.

'So I thought I ought to come and tell you . . .' Alice went on. 'Mind,' she added, in a matter-of-fact voice, 'it's not as if anyone *did* anything to you, is it? I mean, like I said, half of 'em never believed that tale anyway. So it's all been put right now.'

Thanks to Mrs Hayes, I thought. I recalled her rare rages. How Annie must have suffered under her tongue.

I thought of those weeks when I'd lived in fear, of the way I'd avoided meeting people, of the loneliness. And it was all over now.

'I wanted Tommy to tell you that everything was put straight,' Alice said. 'But he said that, for his part, everything *was* straight—always had been, and to let it lie. He wasn't going to bring up such a daft tale again when he'd told you from the beginning to pay no heed.'

I looked at her face, always pale and now pinched with the cold and drawn in lines of misery. She stared down at her foot scraping a little furrow in the snow.

'Well,' I said, 'you'd better come in out of the cold. And,' I added, more gently, 'if you could take the children it would be a help.'

'Anything,' she said. 'Anything I can do . . .'

I had the lighthearted feeling that I could stand straighter now, knowing that that particular bit of nastiness was over. True, there had been the word painted on my door, the stone thrown—perhaps by children, perhaps not. I'd never know now, nor did I want to.

So, during the daylight hours it was as if Sirjohn and I were the only two persons in the world. I knew that it could not last, but I looked for nothing beyond the day. And, although I wanted him better, healed and well again, I could only count those days of tender, friendly, passionless love as a gift and be grateful while they lasted.

They lasted for four days. Then, as if the gods wished to bring us to heel, the fever began. I had dozed in my chair one evening and awoke to find that the candle was guttering and the fire was almost dead. The room had grown chilly, but Sirjohn's hands were hot. He murmured a little in sleep, and I spoke to him. I tried to make him take a drink, but he pulled away fretfully.

After that, each day was worse than the one before as I watched his hands pick and pluck at the covers, listened to the confused tumble of words. 'Go . . . to the back door, and ask for Mrs Broome. January—in the lane. And she smiled at me—such a smile. I cannot think why Olivia should displease you so, my dear, unless it is because she pleases me; it was ever thus. But no matter. It is not important—tonight I shall ride to Almongate . . . "And bid haste the evening star on his hill top, to light the bridal lamp." My bride has no dowry—it will be my pleasure to endow her. Freehold and ninety acres to the west, arable and pasture . . . right of pannage. If you will see to that, Mr Gosling, I shall be infinitely obliged to you. All tied up, legal and proper. She should not grub in the earth . . . She dances with a pretty grace . . .'

'Hush,' I would whisper. 'Please, no more. You must rest. Please.'

His face would turn to the wall and back again, his

eyes wide, staring but not seeing. 'Tonight I shall go
to Almongate. Yes, I will take her a book. Sometimes
one must borrow from books . . . "For God's sake hold
your tongue and let me love." No more talk, Hester.
Hester! Where is she?'

'Ssh, I'm here.' He'd sit up, wild-eyed, grunting with
the pain of his movement, and I'd try to press him
down again, to cover him. 'I'm here, my love. Oh,
please be still . . . rest.'

'I shall ride to Almongate tonight.'

On and on it went: words pouring out, words that
meant nothing to me, and words that meant everything, in a voice now grown hoarse. I sent for the
doctor who came and bled him and went away, telling
me that the fever must run its course.

There was nothing I could do except sit with him,
trying to draw the heat from his body with cool cloths,
trying to coax a little liquid into his mouth, trying not
to listen as he, from that far-off place where his fever
had taken him, spoke of his life and his love and recalled in heartbreaking detail the hours we'd spent
together.

The fever went on into the ninth day. Now his voice
was little more than a whisper, a cracking of the air.
The noise of his breathing filled the room, seeming to
rend his body, while his hands, as if possessing a
separate life of their own, worried the covers like two
distressed, gnawing animals. He called my name again
and again, and I couldn't make him understand that I
was with him. I couldn't reach him. He had gone from
me.

I watched the covers turn dark with his sweat; I
washed him with cool water, laid cold cloths on his
head and then I lay beside him and held him, hoping
that, somehow, he knew I was with him and was glad
of me. I stayed for a time trying to will the heavy stillness of my body into his. Then, gradually, I became
aware of a strange tranquillity. It was as if soft wings
had passed through the sick air, hushing the noise of

his breathing, silencing his broken words. Fearfully I lifted my head and listened. The room was filled with a sense of peace. Gently I touched his forehead; it was cool and moist, and his hands rested at last. He breathed quietly in sleep. It was over. The fever had broken.

I too, slept then, and when I awoke he was watching me. We lay for a time in silence, speaking to each other with only our eyes, then he whispered: 'Before God, I will not let you go again. I will not. I lost you. Where were you?'

'I was here with you. I would never leave you.'

'Will you be with me always? Will you, Hester? Not only in my thoughts but in my life, my days?'

'Hush,' I whispered, wondering if there were still a trace of fever left. 'You must rest.'

'Then we will speak of it again. Stay with me.'

The days passed. Neither of us talked much, feeling no need for words. Then, one afternoon, when he was sitting by the window, he said: 'Now we must talk. I'm rested, and tomorrow I must go back to the Old Hall.'

Beyond the snow-clouded fields the dark yews, the old cedars that screened the Hall showed clearly. I did not want to think of tomorrow.

'Hester, I want you to come away with me. No,' he held up a hand as I began to speak, 'you must think carefully. You have your land and Almongate now. You are secure. When I went to see Mr Gosling I was thinking that life would go on as it had in the past, that I would visit you, get to know my child, feel that my home was here with you even though my place was at the Old Hall. But that was before . . . And then, when I awoke that morning after the fever, I lay looking at you, and I knew that this was the way it should be. We cannot return to what is gone— letting our lives touch for a few hours, then parting, living separately. We belong together. But, for the first time in your life, your future is safe. You have

your land, and I know that it means much to you. Can
I now ask you to give it up and come with me? You
must think carefully.'

I went to stand behind him, to look out across the
land that belonged to me, and I put my hand on his
shoulder. His hand came up and covered it. And I
thought: You are the root of my being. You are the
taste on my tongue, the light in my eye, even the beat
of my heart . . . And you ask me to think carefully!

Aloud I said: 'I do not have to think.'

Then he went back to his home. There was much for
him to oversee, he told me, settlements and arrangements to be made, and little time in which to do it all
because we both wanted to be away from here before
the baby was born.

The snow began to melt, clinging crystal-fringed in
the hollows round the tree roots, in the ditches, against
the north side of Almongate, gradually seeping away
under a mild, damp sky. I wrapped up the children
warmly and took them to walk over our land. When
we reached the river-bank I turned to look back at
Almongate: my home with its crinkled orange roof,
the corner by the fire where Sirjohn had waited for me
on the night that Matthew died, the room where Livvy
was born. And there was too, the garden that had
meant so much to me, the pear tree under which Daniel had filled his jar with earth and, laughing, made
crumbling heaps. There was the feel and smell, the
very flavour of the place. I would not sell it, and I
could not walk away and leave it. It should be used
and cared for. I walked back slowly.

In the garden Tommy was sawing logs. 'Tommy,' I
said, 'when you've done do you think you could find
Jack Hallam. I'd like to see him.'

When he came I cut him a slice of bacon and raked
a potato from the embers. 'I'll talk while you eat,' I
said. Then: 'Why did you never marry, Jack?'

His eyebrows shot up to meet the silver-gilt hair.

'I'm not asking idly. I have a reason.'

'Well,' he said, putting down his knife, 'I'm no prize, am I? No steady job, and I couldn't ask a girl like Annie to share two rooms with my mother and seven brothers and sisters, could I?'

'A girl like Annie,' he'd said. Love does that.

'But if you had a steady job and a cottage, would you marry her then?'

'Right away,' he said. 'And pigs might fly.'

'Well, then,' I said and began to talk.

After he'd gone I started to gather a few things together as if I were hurrying time along. I picked up the porcelain inkpot and stood holding it, remembering the evening when Sirjohn had given it to me, saying, 'A good scholar merits good tools,' and there was the painted scent flask, and I recalled the night he'd brought it, remembered him pouring a little into his palm and passing it over my neck, my shoulders . . . These things I would take: they belonged to the future as well as the past. The furniture I would leave for Annie and Jack.

We'd talked until we were almost hoarse and Jack was lightheaded, either from the ale he'd drunk or with the prospect before him. At first I'd felt a little as God must feel when he metes out his rewards to the good. I'd had little practice at giving. I'd had so little to give in the past. And wasn't I giving this man a chance, a home, a job? Wasn't I even, in a manner of speaking, giving him the wife he wanted? And wasn't there, too, somewhere secret inside me, a little grub that writhed and lifted its head and said: 'What better way of getting back at Annie for her talk against you than that you should make her grateful to you?' And I'd managed to smother that thought. Jack Hallam was proud. And I wasn't giving him anything—he was holding my land for me. Annie would tend the house, look to the garden, and she'd do it well.

There would be other things to talk about before I left. I must make sure that Jack would employ Tommy.

I would ask him to keep the shelter by the bridge in good repair. I must talk to him about winter wages. Many farmers paid their labourers less during the bad months; this caused hardship at a time when living was not cheap. I did not want that to happen to any man who worked on my land.

I took paper and quill from the cupboard and began to make a list of the things I must speak to Sirjohn about. And perhaps Mr Gosling would write some kind of agreement so that both Jack and I knew just what was expected of each of us, for, one day perhaps, my children would come back here.

'Come,' I said to them now, 'to bed. Soon we'll be going on a long journey.'

'With horses?' Daniel asked. I bent and kissed him. Matthew's son, all right. 'Yes, with horses. We shall travel in good style.' I hugged them for a moment before I left them.

Then I sat down to write to Olivia. I had had a long letter from her two days ago, thanking me for my care of her father.

'He has told me that you are leaving Stoke Friary together,' she had written. 'Many times I have wished that my father could have known one small part of the joy my marriage has brought me. Now I need wish no longer, and I cannot fully describe the happiness with which I received his news.'

She went on to say that she had visited Roland who, with Miss Goodbody, was now lodged in a large house only a few miles from her own home. 'It is a pleasant place, run by kindly people, and the patients there—although in the strictest sense of the word they are not ill—appear to be happy and well cared for. Roland has made a friend there, and Miss Goodbody looks much better than when she arrived and is putting on flesh. She confided to me that she was relieved not to have the sole charge of Roland, and she is highly satisfied with the situation.

'I have had a letter from my mother which said neither more nor less than I expected. She has taken the lease of a house in Bloomsbury to be close to her sister, finding London far more agreeable than Stoke Friary which, she writes, she always regarded as intolerably dull and unfriendly, and she is pleased at last to put those "excessively unhappy years" behind her. Dominic and his wife are to live with her, and that appears to be all she wants. But much of this my father will have told you.

'I feel rather sad that the Lindseys are leaving the village after so many generations of them have lived there. I did not find my years in Stoke Friary "excessively unhappy". Indeed I had much happiness, as did you, dear Hester. But when you are established in your new home (and it's a dear little house; it belonged to my father's aunt, as you will know, and I stayed there sometimes as a child, before she died), I shall visit you. Our children will play together and we will talk. Warwickshire is not so very much farther away. We will meet often.'

There was not much that I could tell her in my letter—the last one I would write in this house—except to thank her for her good wishes and say with what pleasure I would look forward to seeing her again.

I signed my name at the end feeling a renewal of the old pleasure as the words crept from the quill, then I stood up to ease the cramp in my back. I went across to the window to close the curtains.

A west wind had arisen, dragging huge, milky clouds across the stars. Behind me would be that strange bar of light that is the river at night, whilst ahead was the Old Hall and Sirjohn; soon he would come to tell me of our arrangements for leaving.

In the years to come my cattle would be cropping the pasture, my crops would come to harvest and my pigs fatten. 'To everything there is a season.' It was the pattern of life, and it was written so. My season

here had held everything: birth and death, seedtime,
bloom and harvest. All of living in a three year
season.

I felt the child stir within me. Soon it would fill
my arms. Soon we would be together, all of us: the
people whom I loved most—my children and *his* child,
and he at the very centre. In an hour or two he would
come to me and say: 'Hester, we go tomorrow, or on
Friday, or next week.' What did it matter when, because for the rest of our lives we would be together.

I slid back the window a little, and the gentle, fresh
wind drifted over my face. It had the softness, the
damp shyness of spring in it, and for a moment I
fancied that in the darkness by the corner of the
house the little patch of aconites shone gold like a
pool of sunlight. A line of a song which Olivia had
taught me came into my mind, the words written in
the style of another age: 'Sumer is icumen in . . .'

Summer. High summer. The high summer of my
life was before me.

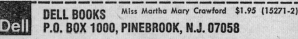

*A Sizzling Novel of a
Powerful and Troubled Family*

RICH FRIENDS

By JACQUELINE BRISKIN

A chilling, uniquely Californian tale of one family's
tragedy from 1946 when the future seemed golden, to
1975, when the bright sun cast a long shadow on a
breeding ground of sordid sex, brutalizing drugs and
murderous cultism.

Here is an unforgettable saga of men and women, parents
and children, whose money, looks, talent, and ambition
could not save them from menace, violence and ultimate
tragedy.

"A superbly told tale!"   —*Chattanooga Times*

"Tragedy and violence erupting in the sunshine . . .
engrossing, well-told and powerful."

—*Louisville Courier-Journal*

A DELL BOOK $1.95